The Silver Squad Rides Again

MARTY ESSEN

Encante Press, LLC
Victor, MT
Books@EncantePress.com
SAN: 850-4326

Cover design by: Laura Duffy, Laura Duffy Design
Interior layout by: Deborah Bradseth, DB Cover Design

Publisher's Cataloging-in-Publication Data

Names: Essen, Marty, author.
Title: The silver squad rides again / Marty Essen.
Description: Victor, MT : Encante Press, 2026. | Summary: The further adventures of the Silver Squad.

Identifiers: LCCN 2025927106 | ISBN 9798994260708 (pbk.) | ISBN 9798994260715 (epub)
Subjects: LCSH: Love in old age – Fiction. | Vigilantism – Fiction. | Older people – Travel – Fiction. | Animal welfare – Fiction. | Homeless persons – Protection – Fiction. | BISAC: FICTION / Romance / Later in Life. | FICTION / Romance / Action & Adventure. | FICTION / Crime.
Classification: LCC PS3605.S64 2024 | DDC 813 E--dc23

10 9 8 7 6 5 4 3 2 1

Also by Marty Essen:

Cool Creatures, Hot Planet: Exploring the Seven Continents

Endangered Edens: Exploring the Arctic National Wildlife Refuge, Costa Rica, the Everglades, and Puerto Rico

Time Is Irreverent

Time Is Irreverent 2: Jesus Christ, Not Again!

Time Is Irreverent 3: Gone for 16 Seconds

Time Is Irreverent: Ooh, It's a Trilogy! (Books 1-3)

Hits, Heathens, and Hippos: Stories from an Agent, Activist, and Adventurer

Doctor Refurb

The Silver Squad: Rebels With Wrinkles

CONTENTS

For Natalie

CHAPTER 1

Aaron's Story, Part 1

Aaron Anderson picked crumbs out of his scraggly brown beard as he lay on his side next to a small campfire he'd built near the Mississippi River. He knew someone from the Minneapolis Police Department would show up in a week or two, forcing him to move again, but as homeless camps went, this one was better than most. He had easy access to water, a gentle breeze kept the stench of his wall-less outhouse at bay, and he'd learned to ignore the trash. Eventually, some do-gooder group of environmentalists would swoop in to clean up the place anyway.

Even though he didn't consider the current day a good day, at least it wasn't as miserable as some were. His last good day and first in a long series of miserable days both happened on the same date a little over a year ago, in October. That day began in a promising way with a promotion at work. It wasn't a huge promotion, but it was big enough to allow him to move up to a better brand of whiskey and to bet more aggressively during his Friday night poker games. Best of all, it would, at least temporarily, stop his wife's incessant nagging that he pay their bills on time and put a little into savings.

That good day changed abruptly when he arrived home and noticed a shiny black Mustang parked in front of his house. He had recognized the car from the previous night, when its gray-haired driver spied on him through his kitchen window before escaping into the darkness. This time he vowed to make sure the old man wouldn't get away and even chuckled to himself, thinking a little ass-kicking would be a fine way to complete his day.

If only he'd anticipated that the man had a partner.

With a tire iron in hand, Aaron ordered the old man out of his car, unaware that a gray-haired woman was sneaking up from behind. When the old woman tricked him into turning around, the man shocked him with a stun gun. The shock didn't bring him down; it simply made him drop the tire iron. When he turned back to rip away the man's stun gun, the woman picked up the tire iron and knocked him out with a blow to the head.

From there, Aaron's night of terror continued with the old couple driving him to a grade-school playground, where they stripped and zip-tied him, threatened him with worse if he ever beat his wife again, and forced him to drink from a cheap bottle of whiskey. When they finally let him go, he faced a long, cold walk home, dressed only in shredded briefs that left him dangling.

That walk ended prematurely when someone spotted him and called the police. Upon his arrest for indecent exposure and public drunkenness, Aaron proclaimed his innocence, saying that two senior citizens who belonged to a secret cabal had mugged him.

The arresting officers were unconvinced.

When Aaron's wife, Megan, arrived at the police station to bail him out, she'd forgotten to cover the neck and face bruises he'd given her. Or at least she pretended to forget.

Until that night, Megan had endured Aaron's beatings out of fear he would disappear with their children. One glance at him behind the glass gave her all the encouragement she needed to break free of her husband and neutralize his abduction threats. She reported the beatings to an officer, obtained a restraining order, and left Aaron to make his own bail arrangements.

Even though Megan couldn't afford an expensive attorney, she hired an aggressive one who specialized in divorces for battered women. Once Aaron posted bail, her attorney made sure he was only allowed a brief, supervised return home to pick up his automobile and personal effects.

Having been escorted off the premises, Aaron moved into an inexpensive motel close to his office. He hoped his new promotion would allow him to stay there as long as necessary, though ultimately his ability to afford the room would depend on how much and how soon he had to pay two attorneys: one for his criminal defense and another for his divorce. If he could hold out until he received his portion of the assets he shared with Megan, he would celebrate the end of his nightmare by finding a permanent place to live.

That sliver of optimism disappeared when Aaron returned to work two days later. Walking into his office, he found his personal belongings packed into a cardboard box with a termination notice taped to its side.

"I'll fix that bitch once and for all!" he raged as he returned to his car. Whether he was referring to his wife or the old woman who had humiliated him at the playground was unclear—even to him.

* * *

Desperate to save what little money he had left, Aaron lived in his car while he hunted for a job. But with no current references, and an appearance and odor that grew worse by the day, employment eluded him.

He attempted to return home, only to find the locks changed and a police officer in his face within minutes. He considered applying for public assistance, but he'd already been humiliated by more questions than he could stand to answer and, in his desire to maintain some semblance of dignity, refused to ask for something he'd previously mocked others for accepting.

Worsening his situation was that winter had arrived in Minnesota, and living in his car was becoming more unbearable each day. The upper-shelf whiskey he'd been looking forward to when he got his raise was out of the question, though petty thefts and an occasional odd job allowed him to buy enough of the cheap stuff to warm his nights.

Adding to his distress were his weekly calls to his lawyers, which seldom provided good news and inevitably included demands for more money. Then his cell phone provider disconnected his service for non-payment, forcing him to use one of the few remaining payphones in the city. Ultimately, he stopped calling, figuring that whatever marital assets he recovered in court would be sucked up by parasitic attorneys anyway.

By mid-December, the cold forced Aaron to move into a shelter for the homeless. There, the lack of privacy, unstable dormitory mates who talked through the night, and rules that included a curfew, all combined to make that winter the longest and most miserable of his life.

As he saw it, the only positive was the advice he received about homeless survival from those who had been at it for a long time. That advice included identifying the least risky stores for shoplifting, developing pickpocketing skills, locating seldom-patrolled summer camping spots, and learning to barter for almost anything else.

* * *

Come spring, Aaron purchased a used tent and sleeping bag at a military surplus store and began living a nomadic life with some of the homeless people he'd met at the shelter. Sticking together gave them some security, and if the police kicked them out of a campsite, someone always had a suggestion for another they could move to.

Months merged from one to the other. Aaron no longer kept track of dates, but as he retired to his tent earlier than usual, a feeling in his bones told him mid-fall had arrived. He was dozing when a sweet woman's voice called from outside his door, "Hello. I've brought you a home-cooked meal."

Aaron had consumed more whiskey than usual that day and didn't have the desire or the energy to socialize with anyone. Especially if that person turned out to be another Bible-banger, using food as an excuse to preach to him about how he could turn his fortunes around if he just gave his life to Jesus Christ.

"Um . . . thank you," he said. "I can't come out right now. Can you leave it on the stump next to the fire ring?"

"Of course, dear. Is there anyone else in there who'd like something to eat? Another person or even a pet?"

"No, it's just me."

"Okay, dear. I'm setting your dinner on the stump now. Goodnight."

Aaron lay in his sleeping bag, delaying the retrieval of his meal until he was sure the woman was gone. As he waited, the woman's voice repeated in his head: "Of course, dear. . . . Okay, dear. . . . Of course, dear. . . . Okay, dear. . . ."

He sat bolt upright and hissed, "It was her!"

CHAPTER 2

Howling For Justice

"How did deliveries go today?" Barry asked Beth the moment she stepped inside his Blue Loon Village apartment.

"You know that elusive group of campers along the Mississippi River?"

"Yeah."

"They finally moved to a spot where we could access them. There were five tents in all, but no one would come outside to speak with us. We left meals for everyone."

"That's good."

Beth stood for a moment, eyeing the map Barry had spread across the counter that divided the kitchen from the living room. She settled onto a stool next to him and said, "Now that we've reached the campers, I wish we weren't leaving in the morning. I'd like to get to know more about them before the cold weather hits."

"That's why we have an entire Silver Squad team now. There

are multiple people who can keep things running smoothly while we're gone. And if there's an emergency no one can handle, Craig or Tina will call or text us."

"Are you sure you wanna take your Mustang, not my Forester? I've never been to Montana before, but I've heard the wind can really whip across the plains of North Dakota and eastern Montana, and I wouldn't wanna get caught in a snowstorm at the top of a mountain pass."

"We still have plenty of time to complete our trip before winter hits. And if we ever need to make a quick getaway, we'll be glad we're in the Mustang."

Beth lost herself in thought for a moment before saying, "I wish Jenny was coming along."

"She's a busy woman, with a life of her own. The predeparture research she did for us is gonna make our trip run smoother, and if we need further help, she's only a phone call away." Barry pushed up from his stool, disappeared for a moment, and returned with a box that required both hands to carry. The contents clanged when he leaned over and let the box drop the last few inches to the floor. Kneeling, he opened the top and motioned for Beth to look inside. "This arrived via UPS while you were gone."

She dismounted her stool. "What is it?"

"It's a foothold trap for a bear. It weighs over 25 pounds."

She facepalmed. "Seriously? You actually bought this to catch the man who tortured and killed the wolf?"

"Yeah, but I'm no longer sure it's practical. After trying to open its jaws and being unable to budge them, I watched a video on YouTube. Apparently, no one is strong enough to open the jaws without using two C-clamps. I guess I should've watched the video before buying the trap."

"So, are you returning it?"

"Maybe later. For now, I'm gonna pack it in the trunk. If I decide to use it, I'll rewatch the video and pick up two C-clamps in whatever town we're in."

Beth returned to her stool and asked, "If you forgo the trap, what are our alternatives?"

Barry shrugged. "Hell if I know. I assume you're packing our vigilante tool kit. There's bound to be something in there we can use."

"It's sitting beside my suitcase, ready to go. Did I mention that I added disguises for us?"

"No. When did you do that?"

"A few months ago. I knew it was only a matter of time before you found some excuse—um . . . *cause*—to take the Mustang back out on the road. We're not as famous as we were a year ago, but if we ever do something that requires anonymity we'll be prepared."

"What's my disguise?"

"A tie-dyed T-shirt, headband, bell-bottom jeans, and round-rimmed sunglasses."

"You want me to look like a hippie? I'm not sure if that's gonna work in Montana."

"In my defense, I didn't know where we were going at the time."

"I assume you got something similar for yourself."

She nodded.

He continued. "How'd you fit all that into the tool kit box?"

"A kit can have more than one container."

"If that's the case, I want a John Wayne cowboy hat, boots, chaps, and spurs."

Beth rolled her eyes. "How 'bout we see what the locals are

wearing before going too far overboard? It'll be fun. We'll add a shopping trip to our adventure."

"Yeah," Barry said in a sarcastic voice. "Shopping is right up there with jogging on my Top 10 List of Most Fun Activities."

* * *

Shortly after lunch on the following day, Barry finished loading up his Ford Mustang GT. Since he and Beth didn't plan to stay long in Montana, Barry decided to leave his beloved gecko, Gertrude, at home. He didn't want to worry about keeping her warm in the cool weather and instead arranged for someone from the Silver Squad delivery crew to stop by his apartment to give her fresh water and a gourmet selection of mealworms and crickets.

Once the Mustang escaped the metro traffic, Beth looked to her left and said, "Here we go again. Another road trip without a plan."

Barry glanced to his right and replied, "What do you mean? Of course, we have a plan."

"No, we don't. The moment you read that news story about the trapper who tortured a wolf, you declared avenging the wolf to be a Silver Squad cause, asked Jenny to find the trapper's address, and bought a trap big enough to catch a human. Other than that, we know very little about the man. Does he live in a house or an apartment? Does he have a wife? Does he have any kids? Does he have any guns?"

"He's a trapper living in Montana. Guns are a given."

"Still, with so many unknowns, you can hardly say we have a plan."

"We also know that his name is Larry Fucking Miller."

Beth chuckled. "I'm not sure about his middle name, but okay."

"I can't think of a more fitting middle name for that asshole. According to witnesses who heard him bragging in a bar, he hadn't checked his traps for several days. When he did, he found the wolf had all but ripped off its own leg trying to escape. Then, instead of quickly putting the wolf out of its misery, he beat the shit out of it with a bat, wrapped duct tape around its muzzle, and dragged it down Main Street still alive!"

Beth cringed. "I know all that. You don't need to reconvince me that what he did was reprehensible. I just don't wanna travel all the way to Montana and fail because we lack a realistic plan."

"Remember our first caper? Neither of us was sure what to do with the wife-beater we caught."

"Of course I remember. I may be seventy-one, but I have the memory of a . . . a . . . What were we talking about?"

Barry laughed. "That we succeeded by improvising."

"Let's hope we're just as improvisationally lucky this time."

"How about this? If we get there and find avenging the wolf to be too difficult, we'll improvise by turning our road trip into a vacation."

"Yeah, like you'd really drive all the way out to Montana, throw up your hands, and not even attempt to make Larry F. Miller feel the wolf's pain."

CHAPTER 3

Aaron's Story, Part 2

Aaron crawled out of his tent and staggered to his feet. He spun one way, then the other, scanning for the woman who had destroyed his life. He'd only seen her for a second a year ago, and all he could recall was that she had gray hair and a slender build. His memory of the gray-haired man who accompanied her wasn't much better. While those glimpses faded to a blur after his tormentors covered his eyes, his lack of sight had sharpened his hearing, etching their voices into his memory like scars. And their car. He could remember that too. Someday, he'd love to have a beautiful black Mustang like that one.

He stumbled up the trail that zigzagged through the woods. He was almost to the parking lot when he heard a car engine start. It wasn't the low rumble of a Mustang, but there could be many reasons for that. He willed his legs to move faster and reached level ground just in time to see a green Subaru Forester pull away.

He stood there for a moment, wishing he still had his car, so he could follow. Without money to buy gas, insurance, or renew his license plate tabs, he had decided many months ago to sell his car before the cops ticketed it and towed it away. The car wasn't worth much anyway, but then, as a homeless person, his expenses weren't much either. At least the sale paid for cheap booze for a few months and even an occasional sexual favor from a woman of questionable health.

Aaron returned to his tent with purposeful steps. Now that he had a lead, he was already contemplating revenge. First though, he needed to sober up. He grabbed the meal the woman left on the stump, set it beside his sleeping bag, and fell asleep.

* * *

Upon awakening late the next morning, Aaron cleared his head the best he could and huddled around a campfire with two other homeless men. All three exchanged nods but remained silent. That was fine with Aaron. None of them were big talkers, and it wasn't as if anyone's mundane lives inspired stimulating conversations anyway.

Remembering the meal left by the sweet-voiced woman, Aaron retrieved it from his tent, unwrapped it, and returned to the campfire. He took a bite and said to his companions, "Not bad. Do either of you know the name of the woman who delivered this last night?"

"I never looked outside my tent," said the older of the two men.

The younger man poked at the fire with a stick. "Why do you ask?"

"Her voice sounded familiar."

"All I know is that the deliveries come from a group of senior citizens," said the younger man. "And now that they've found us, they'll probably visit us again. Try being sociable for a change. Even if the woman doesn't come along on the next delivery, someone might be able to tell you who she is."

"I'll do that," said Aaron, attempting to hide his eagerness. He nodded to the men and walked down to the river, where he flung his paper plate into the water and washed his arms and face. If he was going to meet the woman who destroyed his life, he wanted to look his best.

CHAPTER 4

Horsetooth

B arry and Beth arrived in the quaint town of Horsetooth after two days of driving. Like other Montana towns near Yellowstone National Park, it featured a downtown comprised mostly of gift shops, taverns, and restaurants. That every hotel and motel in town displayed a No Vacancy sign didn't concern either senior. If they were going to commit a crime in Horsetooth, they'd be better off staying somewhere else.

For now, their goal was to get a feel for the town and to drive by Larry Miller's rural home. Unfortunately, Barry's dashboard-mounted GPS insisted that the address Jenny provided them was located inside a tall rock face on a curve. Even worse, none of the houses near the curve displayed addresses by their driveways.

In frustration, Beth called Jenny to have her recheck the address. This time she viewed the house via Google Earth and led them directly to it.

As Barry set his eyes upon the rundown log house,

surrounded by a leaning barn, a doorless shed, and a yard littered with an old camper and a half-dozen or so dilapidated cars, he commented, "Apparently, the stereotype of an animal-abusing Montana trapper is true."

Beth used her phone to snap some photos of the house and grounds, and Barry saved the location on his GPS.

With their first task completed, they spent the remainder of the evening driving from town to town until they found a mom-and-pop motel with a vacancy. There they reserved a room for three days, anticipating it would give them enough time to avenge the wolf and, if that went well, take a trip south into Wyoming for a Yellowstone National Park visit.

* * *

Barry and Beth awoke the following morning with plans to spend part of the day conducting surveillance. As they soon learned, surveillance in rural Montana is more difficult than it is in a city, where they could simply park on the street and observe from a car. Here, parking on the gravel road in front of Larry's house would inevitably draw attention. So instead of parking, they drove by every ten minutes, accompanied by Barry's near-continuous grumbling about the dust accumulating on his shiny car.

From those drive-bys, they deduced that Larry was likely at work or staying indoors. If the latter, he was wise to be cautious. The story of his brutal wolf-torture had made national news, transforming him from an obscure trapper into a notorious villain.

When Barry pulled onto the shoulder a little past Larry's house, Beth picked up her smartphone and dialed Jenny. "Hey,

Jen. Do you have a moment to do some research for me?"

"Sure."

"Our surveillance of Larry Miller's home is getting us nowhere. Can you find out where he works? Also, the only picture we've seen of Larry is the one included with the news story. Some alternative images would be helpful."

"Of course. I'll get on it right away. Other than that, how's your trip going?"

"It's beautiful here. If we can avenge the wolf in a reasonable amount of time, we're gonna head south into Yellowstone National Park."

"That's a wonderful idea. You guys deserve a vacation. In the meantime, hit the bars."

"I'm sure we'll do that. But I think we'll wait until we finish with Larry and have something to celebrate."

"No, do it now. News of what Larry did leaked out after he bragged about it at a bar and proudly showed off a selfie video of him with the wolf. I haven't seen any reports listing the name of the bar, but I bet you can find him where the locals hang out to drink cheap beer, play pool, and tell off-color jokes."

"That sounds like a solid plan."

"One more thing."

"What?"

"This isn't a time to stand out. Disguise yourself as necessary and, most importantly, dress like a local. Once you find Larry, I believe your best strategy will be to gain his confidence rather than to sneak up and surprise him."

Beth wrapped up her phone call and looked at Barry. "Let's head downtown. We have some shopping to do."

* * *

There's a distinct difference between dressing like a true Montanan and dressing like a tourist or wealthy politician pretending to be a Montanan. Beth realized that when Barry stepped out of the dressing room in a western store, wearing unfaded blue jeans, a huge belt buckle, a neatly pressed button-up shirt, a bolo tie, a fancy cowboy hat, and brightly polished cowboy boots.

She stared at him for a moment before saying, "Put it all back. We need to find a thrift store."

"Why?"

"Because you have *tourist* written all over you."

* * *

Later that afternoon, Barry and Beth returned to Horsetooth and walked along Main Street, looking more like Montanans than Montana's own governor did. They both sported cowboy hats, boots, and jeans, only now those items looked like they'd just gone through a hard day at the ranch.

They knew the odds of finding Larry Miller on their first try were slim, especially since it was a weekday. With that in mind, the two seniors stepped into the first tavern they came across, ordered a pitcher of beer from the pockmarked man behind the bar, and carried it to an open table near the center of the room.

As Barry filled their glasses, Beth clicked on the latest text from Jenny: *I haven't located Larry's employer yet. If he even has one. I hope these photos help.*

Beth flipped through the photos before handing her phone to Barry, so he could do the same. Larry Miller had spent little time on social media, and since the wolf incident was his first time making the national news, most online photos of him were dated and of poor quality.

When Barry returned the phone to Beth, she said, "Every little bit helps."

"Maybe for you," he replied, "but I've never been good at recognizing people solely from photos—even celebrities. Now that we're dressed to blend in, we might be better off mingling with the locals and getting one of them to assist us."

"I agree."

Barry sipped his beer and wished it was colder before adding, "I think people will be more open to helping us if we pretend to be fans instead of revenge-seekers."

Beth shivered. "That won't be easy."

"The acting or not coming off as creepy?"

"Both."

They stood and approached a young couple sitting at the nearest table. After a brief, somewhat awkward conversation, they moved on to three middle-aged men at the next table. Finding that conversation equally unproductive, Barry turned away, mouthed "creepy" to Beth, and headed for the open pool table in the back.

Grabbing a cue, Beth whispered, "This is a better idea. Maybe we can entice people to come to us."

Even though their pool-playing skills impressed no one, their undercover mission instantly appeared more natural once some patrons put up quarters to challenge. In all, their mingling efforts produced two people who knew Larry Miller lived in the area but hadn't met him, three who had met him but avoided him, and four who were tourists passing through.

Their big break came when Barry handed the bartender his credit card and asked, "Hey, do you know where we can find that guy who was in the news about the wolf? We drove down here from Butte and were hoping to take a selfie with him before heading home."

The bartender studied Barry for a moment before replying, "He doesn't hang around here. Try the Lazy Moose. They held a fundraiser for him a week ago. If he's not there, someone will know how to reach him."

"Thank you."

The bartender handed back the credit card. "Take a right out the door and go two blocks. You can't miss it."

CHAPTER 5

A Pathetic Little Man

A weathered-faced waiter greeted Barry and Beth as they entered the Lazy Moose Sports Bar and Grill. "Are you here for drinks or dinner?"

Barry looked at Beth. When she mimed spooning food into her mouth, he said to the waiter, "Dinner."

"This way then." He led them to a booth in the dining room and set two menus on the table. "I'll be back in a few minutes to take your order."

They slid into their seats and scanned the room.

"He's not in the dining room," Beth said.

"I doubt he comes here to eat. I'm gonna check the other side." Barry pushed out of his seat and looped around the partition that separated the dining room from the lounge. As he scanned the patrons, his eyes widened. Hurrying back to the booth, he exclaimed in an excited whisper, "That was too easy! Larry Miller is sitting with some other men at the bar."

Beth's eyes lit up. "Are you sure?"

"Apparently, I'm better at recognizing people from photos than I thought I was. But check for yourself. You'll see a husky man in a plaid shirt with a bushy beard and that unmistakable hawk nose."

Beth circled through the lounge and slipped back into her seat. "That's Larry all right. How do ya wanna approach him?"

Barry pointed at the enormous TV screen mounted above the bar, partially visible over the partition. "He's watching Thursday Night Football, and the game is in the second quarter. I doubt he'll be receptive to us interrupting him during the game—even if we pretend to be fans of his cruelty. We'll keep an eye on the door in case he leaves early, but for now, let's eat dinner."

Beth grinned. "Are you sure you don't wanna take advantage of him being distracted? You could grab your bear trap out of the trunk and set it beneath his feet."

"Ha-ha. Very funny. Improvisation is our key. I have a hunch that once we introduce ourselves to Larry, the what, how, and where of us avenging the wolf will become clear."

The waiter arrived.

Then dinner.

Then the check.

Through it all, Larry remained on his stool, drinking beer and watching the game. By midway through the fourth quarter, the winning team was obvious, and the men on either side of him headed for the door. That's when Barry and Beth made their move, speed-toddling to grab the unoccupied stools before someone else could claim them.

At first, neither said a word, pretending to be more interested in the game than the infamous wolf torturer between them.

Once the quarterback took a knee to run out the clock, Barry performed an obvious double take between his quarry and the television and said, "Oh, my God! You're the wolf guy!"

Larry straightened his shoulders and replied with a slight slur, "You're confusing me with someone else."

"I don't think so." Barry leaned forward and said to Beth, "Bertha! That's him, isn't it?"

Larry stood, steadying himself with a hand on the bar.

Beth pretended to study the man's face. "You're right, Bart! Imagine that! We were sitting next to a celebrity and didn't even know it."

Barry pulled out his phone. "Sir, can we take a selfie with you?"

Larry craned his head back. "I . . . I really need to go."

"We'll buy you a beer," Beth said quickly.

Larry froze, unsure if a free drink was worth spending even a minute with what he assumed were a couple of crazy old weirdos.

Barry slapped two ten-dollar bills on the bar. "That's for a selfie and a little conversation."

Larry sat back down.

Barry extended his hand. "I'm Bart, and this is my wife, Bertha. I recognize you from the news, but I'll be damned if I can remember your name."

"Larry," he said, ignoring Barry's hand.

Beth gave Larry's arm a friendly squeeze. "We own a ranch south of Butte. When it comes to wolves, we're big believers in the three S's. Shoot, shovel, and shut up! But holy shit. You did it all out in the open. You've got some huge cojones!"

Larry glanced over his shoulder before pointing at an empty

table in a corner. "If we're gonna talk about that, let's move over there."

"What are you drinking?" Barry asked.

"Coors."

"Ah! Just what I would've guessed. Why don't you and Bertha grab that table while I get some beers?"

Larry pulled the tens off the bar and offered one back to Barry. "That's for mine."

Barry pushed out an open hand. "No, no. One is for a selfie; the other is for some conversation. We're paying for the drinks, too."

Larry stuffed the bills into his back pocket. "Thanks, man."

As Larry and Beth strolled over to the table, Barry waved to get the bartender's attention. "Do you have any nonalcoholic beer on tap?"

"Just Heineken."

"That'll be fine. I'd like a pitcher of that and a pitcher of Coors."

Barry carried three glasses to the table before returning to the bar to grab the two pitchers. Arranging the pitchers on the table, he said, "A Coors for Larry, and a Heineken for Bertha and me."

Beth's face crinkled. "Heine—"

Barry squeezed Beth's knee as he sat.

"Good choice!" she finished.

Barry poured the beer and proposed a toast. "To a wolf-free Montana!"

"And one ballsy hero!" Beth added.

They clinked glasses.

Beth set down her glass and pulled out her smartphone. "Before doing anything else, we need to take a selfie!"

The two seniors shuffled around behind Larry, who remained seated. As they leaned down, Beth pushed the shutter icon twice. She also took a picture of Larry by himself after she and Barry returned to their chairs.

"So tell me, Larry," Barry said. "Have you had any difficulties adjusting to being a big celebrity?"

"Big celebrity?" He blew air through his pursed lips. "Try big villain. If you ask anyone other than the folks who live around here, I might be the most hated man in America. Every bleeding-heart liberal wants me in jail."

"Really? Why?" Beth asked.

"They don't understand that wolves aren't welcome in Montana. They kill our elk, our cattle, and our children."

"I understand where you're coming from," said Barry. "But I've never heard anything about wolves killing children. When has that happened?"

Larry downed his beer and poured himself another. "Not too long ago. I saw a video of it on the internet. Some kid was riding his bike along a dirt road when a wolf jumped him and pulled him into the woods."

"So the person filming the attack just stood there and didn't try to help?"

Larry shrugged and took another drink.

Barry bit his lip to prevent himself from launching into a lesson about AI-created videos.

Beth changed the subject before the silence grew too awkward. "I read in the newspaper that you're a trapper. Do you trap any other animals besides wolves?"

"Sure. Coyotes, lynx, fishers, bobcats . . . pretty much any furbearer."

"Do you ever catch dogs in your traps?"

He glared at her. "Hey! I thought you were on my side."

Beth flashed her palms. "I'm sorry. I didn't mean it that way. I'm not a trapper myself and am just trying to learn."

He stared at his beer. "Yeah, I catch an occasional dog. I'm supposed to release them if I can, but those I find alive usually have obvious trap wounds. So . . . you know, it's the three S's."

"You kill dogs?" she asked, restraining herself to a steady voice while resisting the urge to insert the word *fucking* into her question.

"What am I supposed to do?" he protested. "Anti-trapping groups are already a pain in the ass. If the public ever realized how many dogs trappers actually catch in Montana, they'd force the politicians to shut us down forever."

"Is trapping how you make a living?" Barry asked.

Larry shuddered. "I wish. Until the wolf incident, I managed the hardware store down the street. The owner fired me after activists began loading up shopping carts, only to pretend to be shocked by the sight of me at the counter and storm out with screams of 'fuck you!'"

"Do you regret hurting that wolf?" Beth asked.

"Oh, hell no! My only regret is not thinking about who was in town when I opened my mouth about teaching that wolf a lesson. Had I done it during the off-season, with only the locals around, I would've been fine, but I stupidly ignored that tourist season was in full swing." He downed another beer and shook his head. "Stupid. Stupid. Stupid."

Beth resisted asking what lesson he could have possibly taught the wolf, since wolves have to eat to survive, and he killed it instead of releasing it. She switched to a more personal question. "I see by the ring on your hand that you're married. What does your wife think about all this?"

"My wife? That bitch took my daughter and moved to Missoula last spring." He gave his ring a half-hearted tug. "I told her I was sorry!"

"What did you do?"

Larry's lips twitched. "I'd rather not talk about it."

Barry conjured up a sympathetic expression. "It sounds like you've had a rough year."

"That's an understatement." He emptied his pitcher into his glass.

Beth tapped Larry's arm. "Whoa. You were already pretty tipsy when we met. Would you like me to call you a taxi, so you don't have to drive?"

"Tipsy? What are you, the second coming of my bitch wife?" He reclined his head and emptied his glass. "This is fucking Horsetooth. We don't have no taxi service here." He stood, swayed, felt around in his pockets, and extracted his keys. Jangling them in front of Beth's face, he spat, "Thanks for the beer."

He staggered toward the door.

As soon as Larry disappeared, Barry turned to Beth and said, "Come on! We've gotta follow him."

"You're not gonna do something to him tonight, are you?"

"Certainly nothing physical. In fact, I've had second thoughts. Larry's life is already so pathetic, nothing we could do to him would make it worse than it already is." He held open the door for Beth and raised an eyebrow. "Still, we have a moral obligation to keep a drunk driver off the streets."

Beth chuckled. "Yes, it would be irresponsible of us if we didn't at least inform the police."

Staying in the shadows, they followed Larry and jogged closer once he climbed into the cab of his truck.

Barry pulled out his phone and tapped 911. When the dispatcher answered, he said, "I'd like to report a drunk driver. He's about forty years old, with a large nose, beady eyes, red hair, and a bushy beard. He just staggered out of the Lazy Moose on Main Street and got into a beat-up old white Dodge pickup."

"Did you get the license plate number?"

Barry stepped into the street and squinted as the truck drove away. "The plate is really dirty. All I can see is a six followed by a space and a two. I missed the rest. He also has one of those Don't Tread on Me decals in his back window."

"We know who he is."

"So, are you sending someone?"

"An officer is on the way."

"Thank you." Barry returned his phone to his pocket and looked at Beth. "Well, Bertha, I think our work here is done."

"I agree, Bart. Once again, the Silver Squad has saved the day!"

"Yellowstone tomorrow?"

"That sounds like a wonderful idea."

CHAPTER 6

Aaron's Story, Part 3

In anticipation of that evening's delivery service for the home-less, Aaron limited himself to just enough alcohol to calm his shakes. When his soberness led to boredom, he strolled along the Mississippi River to warm his body and stretch his legs. He seldom took such walks but was glad he did when he found a bundle of rope that had washed up onto the riverbank. Picking it up, he visualized restraining the gray-haired woman with it and transporting her to someplace where no one could hear her scream.

As he continued his walk, his thoughts wandered for a bit before clicking back to reality with a plan so good he even surprised himself. During his previous contact with the woman, he had spent much of the time with a cloth bag over his head. And even though she later removed the bag to replace it with a blindfold, he doubted she could remember his face any better than he could remember hers. Also, a year of living on the streets had altered his appearance. Therefore, he reasoned, all he'd have to do is pretend to be friendly and helpful so as not to alarm the woman as he ambled alongside her when she returned to her vehicle. From there, he could overpower her, tie her up, and steal the car.

He looped back to his tent and waited.

CHAPTER 7

Yellowstone

B arry and Beth bought two pairs of binoculars at a store that was open late near their motel. Then, rather than attempting to find lodging in or near Yellowstone National Park, they followed the advice of a store clerk who claimed that tourists had already booked everything closer to the park and recommended they extend their current motel reservation. That would mean a daily commute of almost an hour, but at least they'd have a place to stay.

The next morning, Barry awoke well before dawn. He hated getting up so early, but for the past ten years, 4:00 a.m. was about as late as he could sleep anyway. He shook Beth's shoulder somewhat reluctantly, knowing she didn't have his unintentional early-rising problem. This time, however, there was a good reason to wake her. If they were going to have a chance of seeing wolves as they are supposed to be—running wild—they needed to reach Yellowstone's Lamar Valley by sunrise.

Aware that most visitors never glimpse a wolf, they kept on schedule with a minimum of bickering, entered the park at first light, and followed the Northeast Entrance Road toward the Lamar Valley.

"Watch out!" Beth shouted.

Barry hit the brakes. "What's with all those cars?"

"It's a bear jam."

"A bear jam this early in the morning? Where's the bear?"

Beth pointed at a silhouette out her side window. "There."

Barry leaned forward and squinted. "It's not even a grizzly."

"Are you sure?"

"Yeah. No hump."

"Does that mean you don't wanna watch?"

"I didn't say that. I don't think I've seen more than three or four bears since our high school days in Chisholm. I'm just wondering how many of the people parked ahead of us think they're watching a grizzly."

"Probably fewer than you think. My guess is that most people who are willing to get up at such a god-awful time in the morning are dedicated naturalists."

Barry switched off the engine. "That would also explain why no social media moron is getting out to attempt a selfie."

The bear wandered across the road and disappeared over a hill.

Barry fired the engine back up, and they rumbled on.

When they came upon a long line of cars parked along the shoulder, accompanied by people with spotting scopes and cameras with massive lenses, all pointing across a wide valley, they knew they'd reached the correct location.

Barry pulled into the first open spot he could find, cut the engine, and stepped onto the gravel shoulder.

Beth joined him, and they walked a short distance to where the terrain dropped into the Lamar Valley. Before them stretched a wide expanse of shrubs, grasses, and flowers, all drying up for the winter. While the valley didn't exhibit the vibrant colors of spring, it wasn't bleak, as the shimmering Lamar River snaked through its center and the rising sun cast a golden glow over everything.

Spreading her arms, Beth exclaimed, "This is breathtaking!"

Barry stood silent for a moment, scanning left and right. "I've never seen so many bison in one place. Not that I'm complaining, but the wolves must be out there, somewhere."

Beth pointed. "An entire pack could be just on the other side of that hill."

"Yeah, I know. And if wolves showed up on cue, they wouldn't be wild."

"Then let's simply enjoy the morning. Whatever shows up, shows up."

Barry nodded and raised the binoculars hanging from his neck.

Neither Barry nor Beth saw a wolf that day.

Or the next.

Or the next.

* * *

Following three days of exploring Yellowstone National Park, the two seniors sat on the bed in their motel room, contemplating whether to return for one more day. Barry checked the weather forecast on his phone and said, "It looks like a storm will arrive tomorrow afternoon, with several inches of snow predicted for higher elevations. I assume that means us. As you know, winter weather traction isn't the Mustang's forte."

"Next time we take my car," said Beth.

"Only if we're sure we won't have to do any getaway driving."

"You'd be surprised how much pickup my Forester has."

Barry set his phone on the bedside table. "Shall we head home in the morning?"

She nodded. "Let's hit the road early. I don't wanna mess around and end up racing the storm all the way to Minnesota."

* * *

Following an unsatisfying continental breakfast consisting of preservative-infused pastries and watered-down orange juice in the motel's breakfast room, Barry got to work loading up the Mustang. Large snowflakes floated onto his jacket as he carried the luggage to the car, each one melting on contact. Beth joined him in the parking lot as he stuffed the last items into the back seat.

Smiling over the roof of the car, he asked her, "Did you do an idiot-check?"

"Twice. We've got everything."

"Okay, let's go."

Barry started the engine, shifted into reverse, and looked over his shoulder. A white Dodge pickup filled his window. He paused for a moment to allow the truck to pass. When it didn't move, he tapped his horn. Still looking over his shoulder, he asked, "Does that truck look familiar to you?"

Beth twisted around. "Oh, dear. It's Larry."

Barry puffed out his cheeks. "Are you up for some getaway driving?"

"Um . . . I'm pretty sure we've already been caught."

"Where's our vigilante tool kit?"

Beth shrugged. "The last place I saw it was in the trunk, on the right-hand side."

"A lot of good that does," Barry said sarcastically. "Maybe Larry will let us call a timeout while you dig around in the trunk for our gun."

"We can't be waving a gun around every time we get into trouble. Besides, I doubt he'd be stupid enough to do anything violent in broad daylight. There are too many potential witnesses around."

"Yeah, I suppose you're right." Barry opened his door and stepped onto the pavement. He approached the driver's side of the truck and pretended to be surprised when Larry lowered his window. "Excuse me, but . . . Oh, hi Larry! What are you doing—"

"You got me drunk and sicced the cops on me!" he interrupted.

Barry attempted to look even more surprised. "The cops? How would I even know what you were driving? Come to think of it, how did you know what I was driving?"

"Two old people in a fancy-schmancy black Mustang, first hanging around Horsetooth and now here? I have connections. It wasn't hard to figure out."

"There's no law against staying at a motel and supporting the local economy."

"I don't give a shit about that!" Larry spat. "But because of you and your lady friend, I had to spend a night in jail. Even worse, I was only months away from getting my driver's license back. Now I'll have to wait at least another year!"

"So do you collect DUIs?"

He scrunched up his face. "You're not the big fan you

pretended to be! I know what you are. You're . . . you're a wolf-lover!" He leaned down, disappearing while he pulled a pipe wrench from the floor.

When he popped back up, Beth stepped into view, holding her cell phone at eye-level. "A gentleman from the sheriff's office would like to speak with you, dear. He wants to know why you're still driving."

Larry thrust the pipe wrench out his window, shaking it as he growled, "This . . . This . . . isn't over yet!" He squealed out of the parking lot.

"That's what you think," Barry mumbled.

Beth waited until they were both back in the Mustang before ordering, "Get us home before anything else happens."

Barry did just that. Well, except for a day they spent stranded in a rundown Glendive motel, waiting for maintenance crews to clear the freeway after a worse-than-predicted snowstorm.

CHAPTER 8

Driving Duties

Upon returning to the Blue Loon Village, Barry unloaded the Mustang while Beth met with Craig and Tina downstairs in the dining room to get a report on their meal deliveries to the homeless. Never had Beth left the Silver Squad's volunteer staff unsupervised for so long, and while many of those volunteers once held high-responsibility jobs, she had worried like a mother leaving her house to the care of teenage children for the first time.

Tina pushed her wire-rimmed bifocals up her knobby nose and looked down at the paper she'd set on the table. "While you were gone, we delivered 107 meals, 33 knitted hats, and 18 pairs of knitted mittens."

"That's the good news," said Craig, running a hand over his hairless head. "The checking account is almost empty, the drivers are waiting for mileage reimbursement, and we only have two days of food left before our shoppers need to make a major run."

"I'll transfer funds from our donation account to the checking account today," Beth said. "Is there anything else I should know?"

Tina stuffed the paper back into her purse and said, "You may want to switch Doug from driving duties. Helpers riding with him have reported some frightening incidents. I don't think he sees very well anymore."

Beth nodded. "I'll take a ride with him and, if necessary, take over his shifts until we find a permanent replacement. Can he cook?"

Tina chuckled. "Not if you want the food to be edible. Meal-packing would be a better choice."

"Okay. Thanks for the heads up."

During the past year, the Silver Squad had maintained a team of three shoppers, three cooks, four meal-packers/clean-up crew, four delivery assistants, and three drivers with reliable automobiles. Additional volunteers contributed by knitting hats, mittens, and other items to include in the deliveries. In all, their food and clothing services for the homeless had gained them national recognition and inspired numerous retirement communities across the United States to copy their efforts.

Because of that, neither Barry nor Beth was as physically involved with food preparation or deliveries as they once were. Beth spent hours on video calls, consulting retiree groups wishing to imitate the Silver Squad. Those imitations, however, were always for their homeless services, never their vigilante services. Barry, on the other hand, was usually the first substitute for anyone who missed a shift because of illness, a doctor's appointment, or a family event. So far, not a single volunteer had quit or died.

As the facility's director, Samantha, once stated in an

interview, "I'm convinced that the residents who can participate have benefited as much, if not more, from this project than the homeless people they're helping. People are happier and healthier when they feel useful, and that doesn't change when someone moves into a retirement facility."

Even though turnover among Silver Squad volunteers was nonexistent, occasionally workers cycled through the various duties. Sometimes the changes were for physical reasons; other times they were to head off boredom. Driving duties, however, were the least flexible. Some volunteers were too old to drive; others no longer owned automobiles. And with Minnesota's winter on the way, every driver had to have a reliable vehicle—preferably an all-wheel drive, like Beth's Subaru Forester.

Winter, of course, was the most perilous time of the year for the homeless. While many would spend their nights in heated shelters, some would refuse those facilities because they had pets or social issues that made staying in such places difficult. Those were the people most in need of the Silver Squad's services.

Beth's cell phone rang. Glancing at the screen, she recognized Barry's number and tapped the green icon to answer. "Hey, what's up?"

"I haven't taken a request since my last day on the air in Denver, but Kate from down the hall rang my doorbell moments after you went downstairs. She has a proposal for me."

"Well, dear, we've never discussed monogamy, because it didn't seem necessary. As you know, I left my second husband for having sex on the side, and that was before I put together our vigilante tool kit."

"Oh, *pleeease!* Remember how I felt like I was cheating on Marilyn the first time you and I had sex after we reconnected? If I can feel that kind of guilt about my dead wife, imagine how

I'd feel about cheating on a woman who's still alive."

"Well, Kate is an attractive woman."

"Is she? I hadn't noticed."

Beth snorted.

"Seriously, her proposal involves a new mission for the Silver Squad."

"Does it fit our goal of changing the world for someone?"

"I think so."

"Then I like it already."

"When are you coming upstairs?"

"It'll be a few hours. I might need to relieve Doug of his driving duties."

"Would you like some help?"

"No. You just drove all the way from Montana. I've got this."

"Call me if you change your mind."

"I will."

He hung up.

Beth returned the phone to her pocket and looked across the table at Tina and Craig. "Is everything ready for today's delivery?"

Craig glanced at his watch. "The road crew should be here any minute."

"Is Doug driving today?"

"Yes."

"Good. I might as well ride shotgun with him and get this over with."

CHAPTER 9

Aaron's Story, Part 4

Aaron waited for days to hear the old woman's voice again. Twice the police forced him and his fellow campers to move to a new location, though he didn't feel that detracted from his plans. They hadn't moved far, and each time the old folks who delivered the meals found them by the following day.

During Aaron's wait, he obsessively fingered the rope he kept by his side, cut back on his drinking, and did his best to get to know those who brought him a daily meal. As part of his getting-to-know-you efforts, he engaged the seniors in friendly small talk that included:

"How are you today?"
"It's so good to see you!"
"How many meals do you deliver each day?"
"Are you part of an organization?"
"What's it called?"
"Every time you show up, you make my day."

"Give my compliments to the chef."
"Did the Vikings win yesterday?"
"Where are your headquarters located?"
"Who's in charge?"

While the seniors were happy to respond to Aaron's conversation attempts, someone had obviously instructed them to avoid providing personal or identifying information. Every time he'd ask something off-limits, they'd change the subject. The most useful piece of information he had obtained so far came from a man who divulged, "We're from a senior citizens' center."

Aaron was unsure whether the man meant senior citizen apartments, a nursing home, an activity center for the elderly, or something else.

After the snowstorm that swept east across the northern states passed through the Twin Cities, Aaron contemplated giving up the wait and trudging west to the nearest homeless shelter. Then he remembered the three joints he had stashed away and the frequent contraband searches at homeless shelters. *Better to smoke them now than risk them going to waste,* he thought.

With that in mind, Aaron added some sticks to the campfire he had started earlier, brushed the snow from the log in front of his tent, sat, and lit the first joint. Alcohol, not marijuana, was his drug of choice, but one night, when he was feeling more self-loathing than usual, he'd taken a man up on an offer of two joints for a blowjob. Three if he swallowed.

That wasn't the first blowjob Aaron had given, nor was it his last. For him it wasn't sexual—"I'm not a fag," he'd tell himself each time—it was merely another form of currency in his homeless survival tool kit.

He sucked in the smoke and held it. Joints he'd acquired while living on the streets were usually of such poor quality that he could barely get high. *Yet another reason to prefer alcohol,* he thought. Still, he was determined to take it easy on the drinking until he'd achieved his revenge, and even a weak-ass joint was better than nothing.

Aaron's body tingled as he exhaled. Perhaps, this once, he hadn't been ripped off. He took a second toke. And another.

Was he worried about paranoid thoughts? How much worse could they be than the reality he had lived through during the past year?

What about the munchies? He had no doubt his homelessness made them worse, as it accentuated the hunger he was already experiencing.

He finished his first joint and wondered if he even needed another. Nevertheless, if there was one thing his homeless situation had taught him, it was to live in the moment. Unrestrained by anything he could think of, he pulled a second joint from his coat pocket and lit it.

Only the roach remained when he heard voices and looked up to see an old man and woman approaching on the path that led to his and some other tents. He recognized the gray-bearded man as the one who had mentioned the senior citizens' center earlier. The slender woman with stylish gray hair was unfamiliar, however.

"Good evening," said the old woman. She smelled the air and smiled. "I bet you're hungry!"

Aaron bit his lip to make sure he didn't vocalize his thoughts: *I know that voice! It's her!*

"I'm sorry, dear," she continued in a friendly lilt. "I don't have any Doritos, but I do have a hot turkey sandwich, a brownie, and a small carton of milk for you. How does that sound?"

This is what I've been waiting for! I can take them both—easily.

He clutched his rope and stood.

He swayed.

And sat back down.

Conflicting thoughts ricocheted through his brain:

She's such a nice lady.
This is my chance for revenge!
I've never heard such a sweet voice before.
That bitch hit me with a tire iron!
But she cared enough to bring me a home-cooked meal.
That bitch put a bag over my head and zip-tied me to the monkey bars!
She reminds me of Aunt Joan. I like her.
That bitch stripped me and left me in the cold!

Finally, he said, "Thank you. I haven't had a thing to eat all day."

"You're very welcome, dear." She handed him the items from the canvas bag she carried. "Here you go."

Aaron unwrapped the sandwich and took a bite. Swallowing, he said, "This is delicious." After a second bite, he added, "Something about you seems familiar. What's your name?"

"I'm B—" The woman froze. Narrowing her eyes, she turned to her companion and blurted, "We need to go. Now!"

The old man tilted his head in confusion. "What about the people in the other tents?"

"Set the food on the ground. Let's go!" She turned and

hurried up the path.

The old man cleared a space in the snow with his boots and filled it with the contents of his and the woman's bags. "Please share this with your neighbors," he said.

"Of course. And tell um . . ." He paused to smile as the woman's long-forgotten name came to him. *Bertha* that I look forward to seeing her under different circumstances."

"Bertha? Her name is Beth."

"Beth," Aaron repeated. He exchanged waves with the old man and watched him retreat up the path. When the man disappeared, he mumbled to himself, "Now we're getting somewhere."

CHAPTER 10

Gecko Rules

"What was that all about?" Doug asked after sliding into the driver's seat and starting the engine.

"I know that man," Beth said from the front passenger's seat. "And not in a friendly sort of way."

"I wouldn't worry about it. When you left me standing there, he obviously didn't recognize you. He seemed to think you were someone named Bertha and even commented with a pleasant smile that he looked forward to seeing you again under different circumstances."

"Oh, dear."

"It's okay. I cleared up the confusion and told him you were Beth, not Bertha."

Beth swiveled toward Doug and glared. "Get out!"

"What?"

"Get out! I'm driving."

"It's my car!"

"Of course it is. We're just gonna switch places until we get back to the Blue Loon Village."

He shrugged. "Okay, boss. Whatever you say. But I don't see why you're so upset. It's not like I gave him your last name or anything."

* * *

Upon reaching the Blue Loon Village, Beth handed the keys to Doug, offered him a little wave, and speed-walked to the elevator. Exiting on the top floor, she hurried down the hall to the last apartment on the left, tapped in the key code, and stepped inside.

She gasped at the sight before her! Barry was sprawled chest-down on the living room floor, his face pointed in the opposite direction. "Oh, my God! Are you okay?" She dropped to his side.

Barry turned his head. "Be careful!"

"Okay," she said, trying not to sound panicky. "What do you want me to do?"

"Not squish Gertrude."

"Gertrude!"

"I'm teaching her to fetch."

"Seriously? Have you ever successfully taught that gecko to do anything?"

"Not yet."

"Why are you on the floor?"

"I thought she might appreciate the trick more if we played at her level." He opened his hand to display three squirming mealworms. "If she comes back after fetching the first worm I threw for her, I'll give her a second one."

"How is that fetching? Surely, you can't expect her to resist eating any food you throw for her."

"Gecko rules. Whether she returns with the mealworm in her mouth or in her stomach, it counts as a fetch. Why get caught up in the technicalities of how she carries it?"

Beth laughed. "Where is she now?"

He pointed. "Still fetching the first one."

She followed his point and spotted Gertrude asleep under a stool by the counter. "Does her return to you have a time limit?"

"We haven't discussed that yet."

"Come on." She stood before reaching down to help Barry to his feet. "Let's move to the couch. We have a lot to talk about. First, I've got to tell you what happened today; then you can tell me about Kate's proposal."

Barry scooped up Gertrude and, after returning the gecko to her terrarium, turned toward the kitchen. "I'm gonna make myself a gin and tonic. Would you like one too?"

"That sounds wonderful."

Working quickly, Barry prepared the drinks in the usual way, with a little more gin for him than for Beth. Moving back into the living room, he set the drinks on the coffee table and settled in next to his partner. "Now, tell me what happened."

"Do you remember Aaron, the wife-beater from our first caper?"

"Sure. How could I forget?"

"Doug and I ran into him today when we were delivering meals. He's now homeless."

"Holy shit! Did he recognize you?"

"Yes. He was smoking a joint, so it took him a moment. I didn't recognize him right away either. But when I did, I im-mediately set down my food bag and returned to the car. Doug, unfortunately, was clueless as to why I was in such a hurry and stayed behind to empty his food bag and chat. That's when Aaron's brain cleared enough to remember me as Bertha." Her voice grew sarcastic. "But Doug corrected him and revealed I was Beth."

"Did he give Aaron your last name?"

"He says he didn't, but I have my doubts." She paused to think. "My last name likely wouldn't matter anyway. Now that Aaron knows what I'm up to, all he needs to do is get access to a computer and he'll find plenty of stories about both of us. My first name won't help with his search, but it will confirm the accuracy of it. After all, we're not only famous for stopping a mass shooter but also for founding the Silver Squad food delivery service for the homeless."

"What do you suggest we do?"

"I don't know."

Barry thought while he sipped his drink. Then he said, "Besides worrying about security for you—actually both of us—we now have a moral conflict to consider. On one hand, if it weren't for us, Aaron likely wouldn't be homeless. On the other hand, if it weren't for us, Aaron would still be beating his wife and frightening his children. If we wanted to, we could help Aaron get off the streets and put his life back together. But if we did that, who's to say he wouldn't go right back to beating his wife? Or, if his wife has already divorced him, who's to say he wouldn't find another woman to abuse?"

"So do we just let him be?"

"That feels like the best choice. We'll alert Samantha to our security concerns and be careful when we go out. After all, we don't know for sure if Aaron will seek revenge—or if he's even capable of it. Hell, if he was excessively stoned when he saw you, he might even forget the entire thing."

Beth twirled a finger in her drink. "We're learning the cost of vigilantism."

"Can we change the topic to my conversation with Kate?"

"Sure."

"It's her fifteen-year-old granddaughter. She has some kind of genetic syndrome that I can't pronounce. As I understand it, it has to do with a sagging brainstem and an unstable spinal column. The poor girl is bedridden and in constant pain. A highly specialized surgeon can repair the problem, but the health insurance company the mother uses for the two of them has resorted to the familiar excuses of calling the procedure 'elective' and 'experimental' to deny coverage."

"And Kate wants us to do something about it?"

"That's kind of our change-the-world-for-one-person-at-a-time mission, isn't it?"

"Yeah, but what can we do? Shoot down the CEO in the street?"

"You mean like what happened to that CEO in New York City? All that would do is get us arrested and give the media something to cover for a few news cycles."

"I wasn't being serious."

"I know."

Beth tilted back her head to finish her drink before saying, "We should meet the girl."

"I said the same thing to Kate, but she proclaimed her off-limits."

"Why?"

"Because she doesn't want to put any unnecessary stress on the girl and, if we do something naughty, she doesn't want the police tracing it back to the mother or daughter."

"I understand Kate's concerns, but if those are her terms, we should pass."

"Are you sure?"

"Yes. I'm unwilling to risk everything we've accomplished based on secondhand information. Besides, American health insurance companies have been denying critical patient coverage for years. To overcome that for Kate's granddaughter, we might have to do something that dances over the edge of legality. And now that we're more legit than when we started out, we need to think about the people we're already helping. Getting ourselves arrested—or worse—would have consequences for more than just you and me."

Barry leaned back and looked at the ceiling. "What if we avoid getting naughty altogether and instead get Jenny involved? She could help us run a publicity campaign, like we did with her last year to oppose private land alligator hunting. That would keep us out of legal trouble."

"I like that. But you know Jenny's gonna require video footage for the campaign. Talk to Kate. Tell her the rumors of our naughty deeds have been exaggerated." She winked. "We might, however, be willing to use our connections and fame to publicize her granddaughter's situation, though we won't commit until we meet with the mother and daughter and shoot some video. Once we do that, we'll confab with Jenny, and the three of us will decide whether to take the case."

Barry nodded. "That sounds like an acceptable plan. I'll get ahold of Kate first thing tomorrow. In the meantime, are you hungry? If we hurry, we can still make it down to the cafeteria before the kitchen closes for the evening."

CHAPTER 11

Kayleigh

Three days passed. During that time, Beth rearranged the Silver Squad's duty roster to switch Doug from driving duties to meal-packing duties. She hadn't personally witnessed him driving erratically, just incredibly slow. Mostly, though, she didn't want to risk Doug running into Aaron again and inadvertently divulging more identifying information. Taking his place was a portly man named Marcus, who was the most recent addition to the Silver Squad. That he owned an SUV, suitable for Minnesota's winters, made Beth's decision all the easier.

Meanwhile, Barry had a conversation with Kate, who had a conversation with her daughter, Emma, who approved without resistance a meeting with her daughter, Kayleigh. From that point on, Barry and Beth would communicate directly with Emma, because doing so would be more efficient than going through a protective grandmother each time.

"Don't worry about my mother's feelings," Emma said to

Barry during their initial phone conversation. "This is about Kayleigh, not Kate."

"She just wants to feel useful," Barry replied.

"I know. And she was useful by putting us in contact with each other. But right now, I'm so stressed, I don't have the bandwidth to worry about anyone but Kayleigh."

"I understand. Beth and I will concentrate on doing what we can to help Kayleigh. Just don't be surprised if we find some way to include Kate, too. I speak from experience about the value of feeling useful during your golden years."

"That's very kind of you."

"When can we meet Kayleigh?"

"How 'bout tomorrow after breakfast? Say ten?"

"All I need is your address, and we'll be there."

* * *

Barry tapped the video icon on his smartphone as he and Beth entered the bedroom. Making eye contact with Kayleigh on the bed, he put a finger to his lips and mouthed, "One moment."

Before anyone said a word, he wanted to let the camera take in the scene, which looked pretty much like any normal fifteen-year-old girl's bedroom. She had posters on the wall, mostly of people he didn't recognize, books stacked on a desk, mostly by authors he hadn't heard of, and shelves crammed with an eclectic collection of photos, glass animals, and other items.

When the camera settled in on Kayleigh, the screen filled with the image of a petite girl with shoulder-length curly brown hair, large stylish glasses, and a mischievous grin. The only items that looked out of place were the hard cervical collar she was wearing and the stack of pillows supporting her back.

"Hi Kayleigh. I'm Barry, and this is my friend Beth."

She giggled. "I know who you are. I used to have a poster of you two all decked out in goth makeup, taken right after you saved all those people from that guy with the assault rifle."

"Used to?" Barry asked.

Her face tightened for a moment. "Well . . . that was a long time ago, and you're kind of out of style now." She pointed. "When my mom gave me the latest Taylor Swift poster, I had to make room."

Beth smiled warmly. "I feel honored to have ever been on your wall. And replacing us with Taylor Swift? I would've done the same thing!"

Kayleigh giggled harder before stopping abruptly to wince in pain. "Sorry," she whispered. "I'm not supposed to laugh."

Beth grasped Kayleigh's hand. "How long have you had to wear that collar, dear?"

"Since I was twelve. I used to wear it for only a few hours a day. Now I have to wear it all the time."

"Are you able to go to school?" Barry asked.

"Not anymore. I don't like the looks people give me when I'm in a wheelchair, and I get dizzy and sometimes faint if I stand too long. Now school comes to me." She pointed to the laptop computer on her bedside table. "I'm lucky to live in a time when technology allows me to attend virtually."

"Are you in any pain?" Beth asked.

"You mean other than when I laugh? Some days are more painful than others. Though I'm kinda used to it. I've also learned what body positions to avoid. Worse than the pain is not being able to do what my friends can do. I'd love to be able to dance."

A tear slid down Beth's cheek.

"Don't cry. I know why the two of you are here. You're gonna be heroes again and force those big shots at the insurance company to approve my operation."

Barry struggled to hold his smartphone still. "We're gonna try, Kayleigh, but we can't promise anything."

Kayleigh reached to her side and picked up her own smartphone. "Can you guys move closer to each other?" She looked at the screen. "And pose like superheroes."

They struck a pose.

"Perfect." She tapped the screen and handed her phone to Beth. "Please enter both of your numbers." Beth did as she asked and returned the phone. Kayleigh looked at the screen and tapped some more. "There. Whenever you doubt your abilities, look at the picture I just sent you and remember you can do anything."

"Now that you have our numbers, can you take a selfie and send it to Barry and me? A picture of you is what we really need to see if we ever have doubts."

She sent the selfie, and the three continued chatting until Kayleigh yawned and said, "It's been awesome meeting both of you. But sometimes too much excitement exhausts me. You don't wanna see what happens if I push myself too hard."

"We understand, dear." Beth held her arms out wide. "I'm giving you a virtual hug."

"I'm not totally made of glass. You can hug me for real if you want. Just avoid my neck and don't squeeze too hard."

Beth joined Kayleigh in a delicate embrace, followed by Barry doing the same. They departed the bedroom and stepped into the living room, where Emma was waiting.

Emma half-smiled—her large brown eyes and high cheekbones making her appear less exhausted than she actually felt—and handed Barry a large manila envelope. "Thank you both for taking an interest in Kayleigh. In anticipation of your visit, I printed up a timeline listing my previous interactions with the insurance company. I also made copies of various applications and rejection notices as well as a sheet that explains Kayleigh's medical condition."

"I'm sure all of that will come in handy," Barry said. "Seeing Kayleigh today confirmed that we have a lot to learn before we attempt to help her out."

"Feel free to call me if you have any questions."

"Either Beth or I will be in touch soon."

Emma accompanied Barry and Beth to the front door, where they exchanged goodbyes.

Neither senior said a word until they buckled their seatbelts and Barry started the engine.

"We're gonna get those bastards," Beth declared.

"You know we will," Barry replied.

CHAPTER 12

Jenny's House

The drive from the Blue Loon Village in Minneapolis to Jenny's house in Des Moines took four hours and three minutes, and since Jenny knew that Barry was obsessively punctual, she was just taking an apple pie out of the oven when the two rapped on her front door and let themselves in.

"So, I hear we're getting the band back together," Jenny said as they entered the kitchen.

"If you're willing," said Barry, selecting his usual seat at the kitchen table.

"The pie smells delicious," Beth said, as she sat across from Barry.

"I'll cut a piece for each of us to eat as we talk. I assume you'd both like a scoop of ice cream with it too."

Barry and Beth both nodded and hummed, "Mmm, hmm."

As Barry waited for the ice cream to cool his pie enough to eat, he slid his smartphone across the table to show Jenny the video he'd made of Kayleigh.

When the video finished, Jenny set down the phone and said, "That poor girl. It's so infuriating to hear that any family could be loyal to an insurance company for years, and then, when they really need them, the bastards refuse coverage."

"So, you'll help us?" Barry asked.

"Of course. Though I doubt a simple video campaign like we did to help alligators in Florida will be sufficient. We're gonna have to back up what we do on social media with interviews and at least one news conference with Kayleigh in attendance. Our actions must create a public relations nightmare for . . . Who is the insurance company?"

"Carephyx Healthnyt," Barry said.

Jenny stepped into the living room for a moment and returned with her laptop. Setting the computer on the table, she opened the lid and typed in a search. "Oh, they're one of the big ones. Fortunately, their corporate offices are in St. Paul. That'll make it easier for public appearances in front of their building, if necessary."

Beth pulled an envelope from her purse and set it on the table. "Kayleigh's mother, Emma, gave us a stack of papers documenting what's happened so far. I haven't read everything yet, but I made photocopies for you of the pages that appear to be most important."

Jenny took the envelope and set it next to her computer. "I'll go through these later." Picking Barry's phone back up, she added, "I'm also gonna send myself a copy of the Kayleigh video."

Their strategy session continued into the evening, frequently deviating into unrelated personal matters, such as whether Jenny was dating anyone, if she wanted to date anyone, and how her media consulting business was doing.

Her answers were, "No," "Eventually," and "Swimmingly."

As usual, Jenny had her guest room prepared for Barry and Beth, ensuring they'd have a comfortable night's sleep before heading back to Minneapolis in the morning. They could have stayed longer, but this time their visit with their virtual daughter was intended for business, not pleasure. Besides, they'd all be together again soon at the Blue Loon Village.

* * *

As the Mustang rumbled north on I-35, approaching the city of Albert Lea, Barry glanced to his right and suggested to Beth, "Hey, we're not far from Austin, do ya wanna take a detour to the SPAM Museum?"

"Are you serious? There's actually a SPAM Museum?"

"Minnesota has a roadside attraction for the largest ball of twine. Why not a museum for SPAM?"

She laughed. "Too bad the cops confiscated the can of SPAM you used to take down the Benny's Country Dancehall Shooter. It could've been a featured exhibit there."

"So, is that a yes or a no?"

"Um . . . no."

"Aw, come on. It'll be fun. We could even buy a can of SPAM at a grocery store along the way and present it to the museum as the authentic lifesaver. They'd never know the difference."

"I'm pretty sure the cans have lot numbers printed on them. They'd figure out in a second that the can we presented was too new."

Barry stuck out his lower lip in a mock pout.

Beth shot him a lopsided grin. "You really want to go to the SPAM Museum, don't you?"

He nodded.

"Okay, but if I agree to go, you must promise you'll never make us visit the largest ball of twine."

"Not even on our honeymoon?"

Beth's eyes lit up. "Barry Swanson, are you proposing to me?"

"No," he said quietly.

"I think you are."

"If I was, would you say 'yes'?"

"I don't know. You'd have to ask me, first."

"How could you not already know your answer?"

"I'm a live-in-the-moment kinda gal."

"So, if I asked, and you said 'no,' I could ask again in a few minutes, and you might change your mind and say 'yes'?"

She nodded. "Uh-huh."

"What if you said 'yes' when I asked? How could I be sure you wouldn't renege five minutes later?"

"I never renege."

"Didn't you renege on your marriage when you caught your second husband cheating on you?"

"That's not the same. Besides, I was relatively young and inexperienced back then. If we got married and you cheated on me, I'd kill you in your sleep. It's one of the advantages of being married to a senior citizen. When someone our age croaks of apparent natural causes, no one bothers with the pesky autopsy."

Barry glanced at Beth before returning his gaze to the freeway. "It sounds like you've put a lot of thought into this."

"How could I not? We already have a virtual daughter together, and I have no idea why I keep my apartment when I spend 90 percent of my time at yours. Sharing our expenses would stretch our money a lot further."

"If we stay healthy, yes. But what happens if you or I get sick? Coverage denials aren't unique to young people, like Kayleigh. Sometimes Medicare refuses to cover medical procedures, too. If disaster strikes, we might be better off remaining unmarried, because only one of us could be forced into bankruptcy."

"Now you know why my answer to a marriage proposal could go either way. Although I can't imagine spending the rest of my life with anyone but you, we're past the point of being twenty-three-year-olds in love and going for it. As unromantic as it sounds, we need to be analytical about whether we continue living together as Satan intended or conform to societal norms and get married."

"We do seem to have the most fun together when we're making our own rules."

Beth slapped the dashboard and pointed. "There's our turn!"

Barry pumped the brakes as he checked his side mirror. "I can't change lanes without cutting off those cars." He returned his foot to the accelerator. "We'll have to visit the SPAM Museum some other time."

"That's the man I love!" she exclaimed.

CHAPTER 13

Aaron's Story, Part 5

As often happens after the first snowstorm of the year, a slight temperature increase melted the snow, creating a muddy mush. As a homeless person, Aaron was seldom clean, and while he'd learned to tolerate most forms of uncleanliness, having his shoes soaked all the way through and caked with mud was something he had yet to get used to. With the three joints he'd smoked long gone, the mellowness he felt when meeting the woman responsible for his current situation had melted away just like the snow. Even though he couldn't walk away from all his misery, he could walk to a homeless shelter, where he could get cleaned up and sleep in a warm dormitory on a reasonably comfortable cot.

From there, he could walk to a library, get on the internet, and learn what he could about Beth. He knew that a first name, a face, and a yet to be identified senior citizens' center weren't much to go on, but it was more than he had earlier. And if there was one thing homelessness had given him, it was abundant time.

Aaron hid his rope and some other treasures inside the hollow of an old tree and scanned for landmarks as he backed away. Once confident he could find the tree again, he trudged out of the urban forest and headed for a homeless shelter he knew was close to a library.

CHAPTER 14

Throw Pillows

Once back at the Blue Loon Village, Barry and Beth did their best to return to a normal routine. Beth filled in on a food delivery route that was far away from Aaron's last-known location, while Barry substituted for a woman on the meal-packing/clean-up crew who was in Hawaii attending her grandson's wedding.

All the while, their minds worked on ways to help Kayleigh. Although they'd soon begin a social pressure campaign spearheaded by Jenny, they suspected victory would require a variety of tactics that fit somewhere between social pressure and shooting the CEO in the street.

* * *

A week after Barry and Beth's Des Moines visit, Jenny arrived at the Blue Loon Village and moved into Beth's apartment. There she could have some privacy and stay up late without worrying about keeping Barry or Beth awake. Providing the apartment was something Beth was pleased to do, as it temporarily reduced her concern that it had become little more than a place to store her stuff.

Once Jenny settled in and Beth completed her deliveries to the homeless, the two women met up with Barry in the cafeteria for dinner. The usual table, of course.

Jenny took a bite of her pizza and said, "I'm always surprised by how good the food is here."

Barry swallowed a mouthful of lasagna and explained, "Good food is good for business. When I moved in, I thought it was redundant to have a cafeteria when my apartment had a kitchen. I mean, why buy the meal package? I soon learned to appreciate the advantage of easy access to tasty meals that require no grocery shopping, cooking, or dishes to wash afterward. Yet if Beth and I ever want to have an intimate dinner, or perhaps heat up an after-hours snack, my apartment kitchen is there."

Beth added, "I suspect many of the widowers living here never learned how to cook. Without the cafeteria, they'd all be sustaining themselves on frozen pizzas and pot pies."

"Considering that men like me are a minority here, I suspect most wouldn't have a problem finding a woman to cook for them. Hell, if what I hear is true, many of those men now enjoy multiple sex partners." Barry pointed with his nose. "See Kurt over there? That's the third different woman he's had a dinner-date with since we've returned from Des Moines. So even though it's a bitch for a man to have a shorter expected lifespan than a woman, those of us who exceed the averages have advantages."

"Are STDs a problem here?" Jenny asked.

"No," said Barry.

"Yes," Beth contradicted. "Barry doesn't hear about STDs because men don't talk to each other about such things. Similarly, no woman is gonna confess to him that she caught chlamydia or gonorrhea while living here. After all, if Barry outlives me, many of them will want a shot at him. Women, on the other hand, talk to each other about such things. Especially when it involves gossip about someone else."

"I assume those affected get treatment," Jenny said.

"Of course," Beth replied. "That is, once they become aware of their condition."

Barry grinned. "It's good to be in demand." He playfully scanned the cafeteria.

Switching to a breathy voice, Beth said, "But would any of those women you're pretending to ogle get all dressed up and make sex as much kinky fun as I do?"

Jenny cringed and covered her ears.

"Sorry. I forgot about the virtual-parents gross-out." Beth reached into her purse and handed an envelope to Jenny. "How 'bout we change the subject? I printed this up last night. Let me know what you think."

Jenny removed the letter and flattened it on the table. "Nice stationery!"

Barry leaned over for a quick glance. "The Silver Squad has stationery?"

Beth rolled her eyes. "How could you forget? Two days ago, I showed you three design options. I went with the one you pointed to."

"Sorry. Throw pillows."

"Throw pillows?" Beth tilted her head. "What the hell does that mean?"

"Show a man three throw pillows and ask him to pick a favorite. Do it again an hour later and not only will he have forgotten the pillows, but there's a two-out-of-three chance he'll pick a different pillow."

"That's not saying much about men," Jenny commented.

Pushing his plate aside, Barry said, "I don't fish anymore, but I bet if I conducted the same experiment, using fishing reels instead of throw pillows, you ladies would experience similar forgetfulness."

"That depends," Beth said. "Would you be showing me spincast, baitcast, spinning, fly, or trolling reels?"

"Okay, bad example."

Beth smirked. "Did you forget we both grew up on the Iron Range where everyone fished?"

Jenny held up the letter. "How 'bout we discuss the contents of the letter and not the stationery it's printed on?"

Barry pointed. "To the best of my knowledge, Beth didn't previously show me what she wrote. So why don't you read it aloud first?"

Jenny stared at Barry for a moment while she considered a snarky comment that surfaced in her brain. Deciding the comment would only send them off on another tangent, she began to read, "Dear Mr. Thomas—"

"Who is he?" Barry interrupted.

"Edward Thomas is the CEO of Carephyx Healthnyt," Beth said.

"Oh, that's right. I knew that."

Jenny started again. "Dear Mr. Thomas. We, the undersigned members of the Silver Squad, have taken a special interest in Kayleigh Clark, the fifteen-year-old daughter of Emma Clark. Her account number is . . ." She skipped past all the identifying information. "Kayleigh is a bright, vibrant teenager who should be in school doing all the things others her age do. Instead, she is bedridden and forced to wear a hard cervical collar. Even laughing is painful for her. Imagine that—a child who can't laugh. An operation covered by Carephyx Healthnyt can heal her. We know only a special kind of evil would deny Kayleigh a normal life, and, therefore, we suspect that your company's refusal to pay for her treatment is because of some sort of clerical error. After all, aren't cases like Kayleigh's exactly why people get health insurance in the first place? Now that we have made you aware of this presumed error, we trust that you, being a decent person, will order an immediate correction to cover the surgery Kayleigh Clark desperately needs. Sincerely yours."

Barry bobbed his head as he said, "That's a powerful letter. Though I think we should end it with some sort of threat of what we will do if Kayleigh doesn't get her operation."

"No," Beth protested. "If we back Edward Thomas into a corner too soon, it'll just become a dick-wagging contest."

Jenny handed the letter back to Beth. "I agree. Leave it as is. Do you two want to sign before I add my signature?"

Once the letter made it around the table, Beth looked at the three signatures and said, "While the three of us will always be the heart of the Silver Squad, seventeen additional volunteers help with our deliveries to the homeless. I'm gonna bring this to our next meal-prep session to see if anyone else wants to sign."

"That's all good," said Jenny. "But I didn't drive all the way up here just to sign a letter."

Beth dabbed her lips with a napkin before saying, "I think we all know the letter isn't miraculously going to change the minds of the corporate bigwigs at Carephyx Healthnyt.

Consider it a relatively polite opening move we can copy the media on. I'll distribute the letter the moment I get the signatures. In the meantime, let's get right to work on our next step. Something that's not so polite."

CHAPTER 15

The Commercial

By the following day, not only had every Silver Squad volunteer signed Beth's letter, but she also added an addendum to include the signatures of eighty-two additional Blue Loon Village residents and staff. Once finished, Beth used the scanner in Samantha's office to create a PDF of the letter and addendum. Then she mailed the originals to Edward Thomas and emailed copies to the local and national media contact list Jenny had compiled.

With their opening move completed, the Silver Squad began work on a social media campaign, which they would augment with a targeted advertising buy.

Echoing what they had done a year earlier to protect alligators, Barry and Beth wrote a script. From there, Jenny took clips of what Barry had already filmed, added her own camera work featuring Barry and Beth's narration, and edited everything into what would double as a commercial and social media video.

* * *

[The video opens with a wide shot of a tall brick building before zooming in on Barry and Beth, standing beside the Carephyx Healthnyt sign.]

Barry: Hello. I'm Barry.

Beth: And I'm Beth.

Barry: Ever since we overcame a mass shooter armed with an assault rifle, the two of us, as co-leaders of the Silver Squad, have taken on projects with the intent of making a difference.

Beth: For many Americans, taking on a health insurance company is more difficult than taking on a mass shooter.

Barry: And potentially just as deadly.

Beth: Whether Americans get their health insurance through an employer or the Health Insurance Marketplace, those covered are still at the mercy of faceless corporate executives in buildings like this one.

[Silent video images of Kayleigh fill the screen as Barry and Beth's narration continues.]

Barry: Fifteen-year-old Kayleigh Clark has never met Carephyx Healthnyt's CEO Edward Thomas, and neither have we. Yet, ultimately Kayleigh's future depends on Mr. Thomas or one of his subordinates deciding whether a human life is more important than their corporate profits.

Beth: Kayleigh suffers from a rare genetic disorder that has caused her brainstem to sag and her spinal column to become unstable. She must always wear a neck brace, and her condition has worsened to the point that standing makes her dizzy and laughing makes her wince in pain.

[Video images from Kayleigh's bedroom gain volume.]

Kayleigh [laughs and winces]: Sorry. I'm not supposed to laugh.

Beth [grasps Kayleigh's hand]: How long have you had to wear that collar, dear?

Kayleigh: Since I was twelve. I used to wear it only for a few hours a day. Now I have to wear it all the time.

Barry: Are you able to go to school?

Kayleigh: Not anymore. I don't like the looks people give me when I'm in a wheelchair, and I get dizzy and sometimes faint if I stand too long. Now school comes to me. [She points to the laptop computer on her bedside table.] I'm lucky to live in a time when technology allows me to attend virtually.

Beth: Are you in any pain?

Kayleigh: You mean other than when I laugh? Some days are more painful than others. Though I'm kinda used to it. I've also learned what body positions to avoid. Worse than the pain is not being able to do what my friends can do. I'd love to be able to dance.

[The camera focuses on a tear sliding down Beth's cheek, then returns to Kaleigh.]

Kayleigh: Don't cry. I know why the two of you are here. You're gonna be heroes again and force those big shots at the insurance company to approve my operation.

Barry: We're gonna try, Kayleigh, but we can't promise anything.

Kayleigh [Reaches to her side and picks up her smartphone.]: Can you guys move closer to each other? And pose like superheroes. Perfect. [A photo of Barry and Beth fills the screen as Kayleigh's voice continues.] Please enter both of your phone numbers. There. Whenever you doubt your abilities, look at the picture I just sent you and remember you can do anything.

[Video resumes.]

Beth: Now that you have our numbers, can you take a selfie and send it to Barry and me? A picture of you is what we really need to see if we ever have doubts.

[Kayleigh's selfie fills the screen for a moment, then the video picks up at the point where she yawns.]

Kayleigh: It's been awesome meeting both of you. But sometimes too much excitement exhausts me. You don't wanna see what happens if I push myself too hard.

Beth: We understand, dear. [She holds her arms out wide.] I'm giving you a virtual hug.

Kayleigh: I'm not totally made of glass. You can hug me for real if you want. Just avoid my neck and don't squeeze too hard.

[As Beth joins Kayleigh in a delicate hug, the video freezes.]

Barry [Speaks over the still image.]: Mr. Thomas, it's within your power to change Kayleigh's life. Let her dance! Please approve the operation she so desperately needs.

["Call Carephyx Healthnyt now! Ask Edward Thomas to help Kayleigh," fills the screen with the phone number.]

* * *

Once the commercial satisfied everyone, Jenny backed it up but didn't post it. As difficult as it would be for them to wait, they needed to give Edward Thomas sufficient time to respond to their letter. In the meantime, Jenny returned to Des Moines to take care of her cats and continue the projects she was working on as a freelance media consultant.

Barry and Beth also returned to their normal activities. With Minnesota's winter moving in, finding and feeding the homeless each day was about to get more difficult.

* * *

A week passed without a response from anyone at Carephyx Healthnyt. Beth texted Jenny: *Begin ad campaign.*

CHAPTER 16

Aaron's Story, Part 6

During the same time the Silver Squad was advocating for Kayleigh, Aaron was staying at a shelter near the library and trying to get his life back together. For the first time in over a year, he'd gone multiple days without drugs or alcohol. He even got a haircut and secured a part-time job at a warehouse.

When Aaron lost his wife, kids, and job—"All because of that bitch Beth and that gray-haired guy"—he'd lost all enthusiasm for life. Deep down, he knew he was partly to blame for his predicament. After all, he couldn't deny that he'd hit his wife on multiple occasions. Being homeless didn't have to be forever, however, and his newfound prospect for revenge had given him a sense of purpose he hadn't felt since that fateful night when Beth and her companion stripped and humiliated him at that grade-school playground.

Aaron was surprised by just how useful a common first name could be in locating one person among the more than three million who lived within the Twin Cities metropolitan area. While sitting in a cubical at the library, he'd entered a simple internet search using the terms *Beth* and *senior citizen food delivery to the homeless* that brought up multiple local newspaper articles featuring photos of the woman and her companion, Barry Swanson. Now he knew the man's name, too. And since those articles mentioned that both had engaged the residents of the Blue Loon Village in delivering food and knitted clothing to the homeless, he also knew where they lived. *How convenient that they're famous!* he thought. *Why hadn't I tried this earlier?*

The main problem, as Aaron saw it, was that he was too far away from the Blue Loon Village to walk there. He needed to find transportation and, if possible, an apartment or a loft he could rent.

At his job later that afternoon, he asked the warehouse supervisor if he could use the old black phone that was mounted on the back wall. "Make it quick," the supervisor said.

Aaron dialed Gunther Lee, the attorney who had been handling his divorce. They hadn't spoken in eight months, so he was surprised when the secretary put him right through. Even more surprising was the relief he heard in Gunther's voice.

"I'm so glad you called," Gunther began, launching into details that included the sale of Aaron and Megan's house as well as the liquidation of the personal assets Aaron had left inside the house, all of which a judge approved when no one could find him.

"They can do that?" Aaron asked, unsure if he should be happy or angry.

"As far as anyone knew, you were dead or living in another country. When an offer came in for the house that was above market value, Megan, her attorney, and I all agreed that it was in the best interest of everyone to accept it."

"So where's my money?"

"I'm holding it in an account for you. When can you come by my office to sign the paperwork?"

"How much is there?"

"I don't know the exact figure off the top of my head. The attorney who got your criminal charges dropped put in a claim, and of course, you must pay my bill in full too. But once you sign everything I have for you, you'll leave my office a single man with more money in your pocket than I suspect you've had in quite a while."

Aaron didn't believe for a second that Gunther didn't know how much money was waiting for him. Then again, coming into any money was the best news he'd heard in more than a year. "It's probably easiest if you name the time. I don't exactly have a tight schedule to keep."

"I'm free tomorrow at four-fifteen. How does that sound?"

"I'll see you then." Aaron hung up.

CHAPTER 17

Aaron's Story, Part 7

Aaron showered at the shelter, put on a clean shirt he'd picked up at a thrift store, and caught a bus that stopped within two blocks of his attorney's office. Walking the rest of the way, he arrived only a few minutes late.

He entered a tiny stucco building that had been built in the 1930s. Only the interior appeared to have been updated. The front room served as a reception area and office for the legal secretary, and behind her desk, a little to the right, was a door leading to Gunther's office.

Even though Gunther knew that Aaron had arrived, he still waited for his secretary to go through the motions of announcing the appointment.

Once the formalities were out of the way, the portly attorney walked into the reception area, shook Aaron's hand, and escorted him into his office. There, Gunther motioned for Aaron to take the low-back chair facing his desk before plopping into his own high-back leather chair on the opposite side.

Wasting no time on small talk, Gunther took a paper-clipped collection of pages from a wire basket on the far side of his desk and held them out to Aaron. "Considering all that has happened, I think you'll be pleased."

Aaron set the papers on the edge of the desk, scooted his chair forward, and began to read. "Fourteen thousand dollars!" he exclaimed when he reached the second-to-the-last page. "That's all I get for half of my house and everything I owned inside it?"

"The mortgage you had to pay off took a chunk of it. Look on the bright side. You'll be free and clear both financially and maritally."

"What about alimony or child support?" he asked.

"That's still unsettled. Megan's attorney has provided an addendum stating that if you agree to give up your parental rights and never contact Megan again, she won't seek either form of support."

"And if I reject the addendum?"

"Your support will be based on your income, which I suspect isn't much at this time. But if you turn your life around, you can count on her revisiting the issue."

"So, to totally finish this, do we have to have a meeting with Megan and her attorney or go in front of a judge or anything?"

"That depends on you. I did my best to stall and negotiate on your behalf. But your disappearance tied my hands. While I can't reverse the sale of the house, you're certainly within your rights to reject the divorce paperwork, explain your disappearance to the judge, and request to renegotiate. Needless to say, if you'd like me to handle that for you, I'll have to withhold a portion of your fourteen thousand dollars as a retainer.

Otherwise, you can sign the divorce papers and either accept or reject the addendum."

"You attorneys had it all worked out among yourselves," Aaron scoffed. "Everyone gets a piece of me."

Gunther shrugged and slid a pen across his desk. "You should be glad we worked it out. Had we engaged in a protracted fight, your check would've been a lot smaller."

Aaron puffed out his cheeks. "Let's get this over with. Where do I sign?"

Gunther pointed. "Here, here, and here. That will take care of everything but the addendum." He pulled another paper-clipped document from his wire basket and pushed it across his desk. "This is the addendum. If you approve, we'll add it to the contract."

"Once I sign, how soon will I get my money?"

"I can cut you a check immediately."

Aaron scanned the addendum and asked, "Do you have anything to drink that's harder than water?"

"I think I can find something," Gunther said with a wink. Pushing up from his chair, he stepped over to an antique cellarette, filled two small whiskey glasses, handed one to Aaron, and carried the other to his desk.

After downing his drink in a single gulp, Aaron announced, "Okay, I've thought it over. I haven't seen my children in almost a year and have kinda gotten used to the pain." He rubbed his eyes. "Will I be able to see them after they turn eighteen?"

"Legally, yes. Though I suggest you write first to make sure they want to see you."

Aaron signed the main document before glancing at the ceiling as if asking for forgiveness. Looking down, he poised his pen over the last page of the addendum, shrugged, and signed.

"I'll take that check now," he said, sliding both documents toward Gunther.

Minutes later, Aaron stepped back outside, fourteen thousand dollars richer than he'd been in a long time. He chuckled as he walked to the bus stop. Despite all that money, he barely had enough change in his pocket for bus fare back to the shelter.

* * *

During the next few days, Aaron continued reorganizing his life. He began by walking to the nearest bank, where he opened both checking and savings accounts and split the money between them. Next, he visited the nearest used car lot. Knowing he might have to ditch the car later, he purchased the least expensive vehicle on the lot, a Kia K5 with over two hundred thousand miles on it. Now able to handle his own transportation, he drove south to the Mall of America to buy some clothes to make himself more presentable as he began searching for a place to live.

Rather than looking for something in an apartment complex, life on the streets had changed Aaron's outlook. He had yet to formulate a plan for exacting revenge on Barry and Beth, but he knew he'd need to take them somewhere that was secluded. His warehouse job and conversations with people at the shelter had alerted him to multiple old warehouses in the city that rented lofts for various purposes, such as practice space for musicians and studios for photographers. Although many of those lofts weren't intended to be full-time residences, some people discreetly used them as such.

Aaron found exactly what he was looking for on his third try. A band had abruptly moved out of its practice space and left behind a beat-up old couch, a card table with four match-ing chairs, a dented mini refrigerator, and a filthy countertop burner. The bathroom didn't have a shower or a bathtub, but it did have a sunken drain on the tile floor. If he was careful, he could attach a rubber sprayer hose to the sink faucet and shower that way. Most importantly, the space had a lockable private entrance and no other renters around to complain about after-hours noise. He signed a short-term lease, which would be ideal for his immediate needs.

After moving in the next morning, Aaron went shopping. His purchases included a laptop computer and a smartphone with a plan that allowed it to double as a wireless modem. He also picked up bedding for sleeping on the couch, toiletries, and several days of groceries.

Eventually, he hoped to find a job worthy of his talents. For now, he'd stick with his part-time job. Even though the work was tedious, the pay was respectable enough to cover his expenses, and the schedule was flexible enough to allow time off as necessary for revenge.

All things considered, his life was looking up.

CHAPTER 18

The News Conference

When neither the letter nor the ad campaign on behalf of Kayleigh Clark produced the desired results, Barry and Beth elected to move forward with the third part of their plan, which was a news conference featuring Kayleigh and her mother.

Even though both seniors had spoken with the media many times since they became famous, they'd never conducted a formal news conference and weren't even sure where to hold it.

As they tossed around ideas, the first site they thought of was the lobby of the Carephyx Healthnyt building. They discarded that location when they considered how easily the insurance company could eject them from the building or even prosecute them for trespassing. They also contemplated the public sidewalk in front of the building, though they rejected that location when they considered the effect winter weather could have on Kayleigh's health and the media's attendance.

Samantha solved their dilemma by offering to hold the news conference in the Blue Loon Village lobby. They couldn't have asked for a better solution. Located between the main door and the cafeteria, the tall-ceilinged lobby had all the necessary equipment and was a popular facility for dances, games, and other events. "I'll get the maintenance crew to set up the portable stage with a lectern and some microphones for you," she said to Barry when he stopped by her office, "and several rows of chairs for the media."

After confirming Emma and Kayleigh's schedules, Beth set a date for the following Tuesday and emailed an invitation to every newspaper, radio station, and television station in the greater metropolitan area. She also sent a copy to Carephyx Healthnyt's CEO, Edward Thomas.

"Meet Kayleigh Clark!" the invitation began.

* * *

When Tuesday arrived, the lobby looked fabulous. From Samantha's point of view, putting on a first-class news conference was an opportunity to showcase the Blue Loon Village while it was still relatively new. On the previous day, she had instructed her maintenance crew to wash the floors and climb the tall ladder to clean the chandeliers. And timed to coincide with the start of the news conference, she had her kitchen staff create a variety of tasty finger foods and prepare plenty of hot chocolate and coffee, which they set out on a long table with a fancy tablecloth.

* * *

Aaron had also prepared for the news conference. Over the weekend, he had learned of the event by accident. He was visiting the Blue Loon Village website, looking for a directory of residents, when he ended up clicking onto the events calendar page. His eyes widened as he viewed the schedule and considered the possibilities.

The following day he went revenge-shopping, purchasing a variety of items, including an untraceable gun. From his perspective, if there was one good thing coming out of his homeless experience, it was that he had made acquaintances with multiple people who could sell him almost anything.

* * *

The news conference was scheduled for ten in the morning to minimize interference with breakfast and other Blue Loon Village happenings. Emma arrived a half-hour early, with Kayleigh in a wheelchair.

When Beth heard the front entrance glass doors swoosh shut, she looked up, set the script she was reviewing onto the lectern, and hurried off the stage to greet them. "Welcome to the Blue Loon Village!" she said to both before leaning over to give Kayleigh a gentle hug. "Hello, dear. How are you today?"

"Okay, I guess." She flashed an embarrassed smile. "I hate having to sit in this thing. It's mostly a precaution to prevent me from having a dizzy spell and falling."

As Kayleigh spun her wheelchair in a tight circle to demonstrate how it protected her from dizziness, she spotted a man on the far side of the room. He had wisps of messy gray hair, and his frail body jerked ever so slightly to a beat no one could hear.

An electric wheelchair propelled him leisurely toward the snack table. With a few vigorous pushes on her chair's handrims, Kayleigh swung herself alongside him. With a twinkle in her eyes, she asked, "Do ya wanna race?"

The man tried to speak. When recognizable words wouldn't come out, he smiled a crooked smile, pointed to the side of his head, and twirled a finger.

Kayleigh giggled. "I understand. My head's a little screwed up too."

The man pointed at the snack table and held up three fingers.

"Okay," she said. "Girl-power versus battery-power on three. . . . One, two, three!"

The man palmed his joystick all the way forward and uttered a little squeal.

Kayleigh wheeled ahead of the man before slowing and gliding to the table in a tie. Whether she did so out of good sportsmanship or because she felt a catch in her neck would remain her secret. All that mattered were the broad smiles and the gentle high five the two shared before selecting very different snacks.

Armed with a plate full of goodies on her lap, Kayleigh scanned the room and wheeled over to where Beth and Emma were talking. "Where's Grandpa Barry?" she asked.

"Grandpa Barry?" Beth replied.

"If it's alright with you, I'd like you and Barry to be my honorary grandparents. I've never met my father or his parents. So I have a few openings."

Beth leaned down. "Of course, dear. We'd love that. Just so you know, we already have an honorary daughter, so you'll get an honorary aunt with the package."

"Is that Jenny?"

"Uh-huh."

"I've seen her on TV. She's pretty cool."

"She most definitely is." Beth straightened and looked around. "I don't know where Grandpa Barry is at the moment. However, it's not unusual for him to fall asleep at just the wrong time." She glanced at her watch. "Stay here with your mother. I'm gonna take the elevator up to his apartment. I'll be right back."

When Beth disappeared, Kayleigh noticed that her mother had moved off to the side to greet a reporter. Rather than join them, she wheeled back over to the wispy-haired man instead.

As the minutes passed, the lobby filled up. Eventually Barry, who always walked down the stairs unless he was with Beth, appeared on the far side of the lobby. He scanned the crowd, and upon spotting Emma, hurried over to greet her. "Hi Emma. It's good to see you!"

She reached out to shake his hand. "It's good to see you, too."

"Wow! It looks like we're gonna have an outstanding turnout."

"I know. It's so sweet of you and Beth to do this. Oh, a word of warning. Since Kayleigh doesn't have grandparents on her biological father's side—at least that she's met—she's nominated both of you to take their place. Don't be shocked when she calls you Grandpa Barry."

"That would be an honor," Barry said, raising his watch to his eyes. "Is Beth ready? We should begin in about two minutes."

"Didn't she come down with you?"

"No. I thought she was already here."

"She took the elevator up to find you several minutes ago."

"Hmm. . . . I'm surprised I didn't run into her." He glanced around the room. "Maybe she got sidetracked in Samantha's office. I'll be right back."

CHAPTER 19

Gone Missing

Barry found Samantha speaking with one of the residents in the hallway outside her office. He interrupted, "Have you seen Beth?"

She pointed. "Isn't she in the lobby?"

"Not anymore. If you see her, tell her it's time to start."

Barry hurried to the elevator, waited impatiently for it to arrive, and rode it to the top floor. Racing to the far end of the hall, he tapped in his key code, stepped into his apartment, and called out, "Beth?" When no one answered, he backed out and opened the door across from his. Entering the stairwell, he descended the steps two at a time, exited on the second floor, and proceeded past the first four apartments to Beth's door. Once again, he tapped in a key code, stepped inside, and called out, "Beth?"

The lack of response sent Barry back to the stairs and down to the lobby. Finding Emma, he blurted, "Any sign of Beth?"

"No. And we can't keep the press waiting."

"You may have to run things yourself."

"But—" she stopped.

Barry was already on his way to the stage. Reaching the lectern, he peered around at its backside. The sight of Beth's purse hidden on the shelf took his breath away. He knew better than to get lost searching in the black hole only navigable by women, so he pulled the smartphone from his back pocket and dialed Beth's number. Her purse chimed.

"Fuck!" he shouted, loud enough that several reporters stopped their conversations to look his way.

Grabbing the microphone mounted atop the lectern, he slid back the switch. "Beth Potter. Please come to the stage." He knew his announcement would go unanswered, but he had to try. If he panicked and Beth suddenly showed up, she'd give him shit for days.

Barry returned to the floor and joined Emma and Kayleigh, who were waiting by the ramp at the side of the stage. "Something's happened to Beth, and I'm afraid it's bad. Before I tear this place apart looking for her, I'm gonna welcome the media and turn the news conference over to you two."

"What should I say?" Emma asked.

"Just tell your story and open the floor to questions."

Emma shifted her weight from one leg to the other. "I have zero public speaking experience."

"You'll be fine. I'll try to restrain my worries long enough to give you an effective introduction. That way you can keep the formal speech part of your hosting duties brief and concentrate on the less stressful task of answering questions from reporters."

"I can answer questions, too," Kayleigh volunteered.

Barry nodded as if the matter was settled, grasped the handles on Kayleigh's wheelchair, and pushed her up the ramp.

Once on stage, he positioned her chair to face the reporters and handed her the wireless microphone that had been left atop the lectern. Returning to the lectern, he adjusted the height of the attached gooseneck mic and flipped it on. "Thank you all for coming today. I apologize for our late start, but Beth Potter, the cohost of this event and the co-leader of the Silver Squad, has gone missing. I'm her partner, Barry Swanson. Some of you might be familiar with us from our um . . . little incident with a mass shooter in Kansas City a year ago."

He paused when a few reporters chuckled, then pressed on. "Today we're here for a very different reason. In America, most people under sixty-five have health insurance paid for either by themselves or their employers, and of those people, many never have medical claims that exceed their deductibles. But when those claims arise, people have the right to expect their insurance company will honor its end of the bargain. It's unacceptable for insurance companies to say 'no' because the treatment is too expensive or because of some clause they've hidden deep in the fine print of a document no customer has ever read. We the people are tired of the bullshit! An insurance company's first obligation must be to serve those it insures; not its wealthy stockholders."

He pointed. "I'd like to introduce you to Emma Clark and her daughter, Kayleigh. Over the past few weeks, the Silver Squad has been trying to get the attention of Edward Thomas, the CEO of Carephyx Healthnyt. He has the power to override his company's rejection of the surgery Kayleigh so desperately needs."

Barry shrugged. "Need I say that he's ignored us?"

Tilting his shoulders toward Kayleigh, he continued. "Kayleigh is just fifteen. She's smart, funny, and lights up any room she enters. Unfortunately, she has a deteriorating genetic disorder that forces her to wear a hard neck brace, prevents her from standing for more than a few minutes, and even causes her pain if she laughs too hard. So instead of going to school and participating in activities like others her age, she takes classes online and spends most of her time in bed."

He shrugged again and changed to a sarcastic voice. "But hey, as long as Carephyx Healthnyt's stockholders are happy, who cares about the suffering of a teenage girl?"

Unable to think of anything else to add to his rant, Barry turned his gaze to Emma and said, "Hopefully whatever happened to Beth will be something we can all laugh about later. But right now, I'm worried about her and need to find her."

Squaring his shoulders to the reporters, he concluded, "With that, I'm going to turn the microphone over to Emma. She'll be able to give you more information on Kayleigh's condition and their fight to get the insurance coverage she's entitled to. Thank you all in advance for covering their story. Your efforts could mean the difference between Kayleigh being forever disabled or dancing across the stage in a high school musical."

With a nod to the reporters, he exited . . . stage left.

CHAPTER 20

The Trunk

Beth awoke in the dark, her head throbbing. Duct tape covered her mouth, and her hands were zip-tied behind her back. When she tried to sit up, she bumped her head. Rolling onto her back, she kicked up, contacting a surface that gave ever so slightly. Even though she couldn't remember how she got there, she had no problem deducing that she was in the trunk of an automobile. She stopped moving and listened. No road noise. Just silence and cold. She felt around for a trunk release handle, but darkness and the positioning of her hands made her attempt to find it futile.

With her nose running because of the cold, she switched her efforts to the duct tape and rubbed her face against the carpet. When multiple tries failed to entice the carpet to grab an edge of the tape, she wiggled over to a wheel well cover and tried rubbing again. Several attempts later, she could feel that a corner of the tape was no longer sticking to her skin. She concentrated her rubbing on that corner, being careful not to push it back onto her face. Finally, just when she felt her feelings of panic and claustrophobia were about to reach a crescendo, enough of the tape grabbed the wheel well cover to rip the rest of it off her mouth.

Beth gulped air to catch her breath before calling out, "Hello. Is anyone there?" When no one answered, she called louder, "Is anyone out there?"

Even though freeing her mouth had reduced the terror she was feeling, she still needed to free her wrists from the zip ties and escape the trunk. In a rhythm that helped her concentrate, she struggled against her restraints, rested, called out, and repeated. All the while she grew colder. Remembering that the forecast for the day called for a high in the mid-twenties didn't help her mental state, and the lightweight button-up sweater she was wearing did nothing for her numb fingers.

Beth wondered if letting her freeze to death in a trunk was Aaron's way of getting revenge for the playground incident. Moreover, could she even be positive Aaron was her abductor? She flipped through a mental list of alternative possibilities. Ex-husband number one? Ex-husband number two? Jenny's ex-husband? The wolf-killer from Montana? No, no, no, and no. Unless she was caught up in a random kidnapping, Aaron had to be the culprit.

She called out again, "Aaron, can you hear me? Congratulations, you've successfully scared the shit out of me. We're even now. Let me go, and I won't press charges." She waited a moment before changing tactics. "Aaron? There are security cameras at the Blue Loon Village, and I've told my friends about you. When the cops catch you, my frozen body will send you to prison for life."

Silence.

Beth wondered how long she'd been in the trunk. With no lights or sounds to guide her, she couldn't be sure. Eventually, she gave up on calling out and struggling against her restraints. Moving as deep into the trunk as she could, she curled up and concentrated on warm thoughts.

* * *

Gravel popping under footsteps startled Beth out of her stupor. "Aaron, is that you?"

The driver's side door opened and closed.

The engine started.

The car lurched forward, then swerved into a series of jarring potholes. Beth's head slammed against the trunk lid. "You fucking asshole!" she screamed. "You did that on purpose!"

The car accelerated before leveling off at a steady speed, its tires humming. Beth concentrated on the sound, hoping it would calm her nerves. She might have been successful if the car hadn't suddenly veered right and left, sending her crashing from one side of the trunk to the other. Finally, it slowed and stopped.

The silence returned until the driver's side door creaked open and a voice called out, "I'm gonna pop the trunk now. If you've managed to free yourself, this is your only warning not to try anything. I've got a gun."

The trunk popped open.

At first, Beth could only see the black sky and a hint of distant lights. Then Aaron's face slid into view.

"Good evening, Beth," he whispered.

"Good evening, Aaron," she whispered back.

Leaning into the trunk, Aaron grasped Beth by the armpits

and lifted her onto the pavement. "My apologies for the delay. My intention wasn't to freeze you, but I couldn't bring you here until the business below my loft closed for the night. Now we can go inside, get all nice and warm—and you can scream as loud as you need to."

CHAPTER 21

Video Replay

After departing the stage, Barry walked up to Samantha, who was standing off to the side watching the news conference. "We need to talk," he whispered.

"Let's go to my office," she suggested.

Barry led the way and shut the door as soon as they were inside. "I think Beth's been abducted; I'm pretty sure I know who did it; and you can't call the police," he blurted.

Her eyes narrowed. "If someone's abducted her, I've got to call the police."

"If you do, and the cops find Beth and her kidnapper before I do, she and I could both go to jail."

"What trouble did you two get yourselves into this time?" she asked, looping around to her side of the desk.

"It goes back to the Silver Squad's first attempt at changing the world for one person at a time. Do you remember Nadine, who used to live on the second floor?"

"Of course. She's now over in the Memory Care building."

"When we learned that Nadine's granddaughter, Megan, was being abused by her husband, Aaron, we kind of . . . well, let's just say we did something illegal to stop his abuse. And, apparently, our methods were so effective that he ended up becoming homeless. Then, not too long ago, Beth ran into him during a food delivery run, and one of our drivers inadvertently divulged enough information for him to track her down."

"Barry!" She scowled.

"Just give me twenty-four hours." He paused to think. "You've met Jenny Callahan from Iowa, haven't you?"

"Several times. She's a bright woman."

"Very bright. I'm recruiting her to help me. We're gonna search the most likely places Aaron could have taken Beth. In the meantime, are the cameras in the hallways just for show or do they actually work?"

"I'd be in trouble if they weren't always active."

"Check the recordings from the last hour and call me on my cell if you find anything." He turned toward the door.

"I'm not giving you one second over twenty-four hours!" she warned.

Barry pulled his phone from his back pocket as he hurried down the hall. Upon selecting Jenny's name from the screen, he pushed the green icon.

She answered on the second ring. "Hey Barry. What's up?"

"Do you remember the story Beth and I told you about the wife-beater we stripped and zip-tied?"

"Uh-huh."

"Beth ran into him while delivering meals."

"He's now homeless?"

"Yes. His name is Aaron, and at the moment I don't give a shit that he's homeless. The problem is that one of our drivers might've slipped up and given him enough information to track her down."

"Do you think he'd actually—"

"I think he's already abducted Beth," he interrupted. "She disappeared a few minutes before she was supposed to deliver the opening remarks at today's news conference."

"Holy shit! Have you checked both of your apartments?"

"That was the first thing I did. Now I'm searching anywhere else she could be within the Blue Loon Village complex, and Samantha, the director, is checking to see if the security cameras caught anything."

"I'm on my way!"

"Wait!"

"What?"

"Keep your phone within reach and bring your Glock."

"Do you think I'd do anything else?"

"No. But saying it to you removes one additional worry for me."

"I understand." She disconnected.

Barry rushed ahead to check the kitchen, the game room, the library, and the stairway. He even rechecked both of their apartments. He was about to start ringing the doorbells of residents Beth socialized with when his phone chimed. It was Samantha.

"The camera caught everything!" she said.

"I'm on my way!"

Beads of sweat rolled down Barry's forehead as he entered the director's office.

From behind her desk, Samantha motioned for him to stand beside her. As soon as he was in position, she said, "Watch this," and pressed play.

The image of a man appeared on the screen. Even though he was thinner than the last time Barry had seen him and was wearing sunglasses and a knit cap, his scraggly beard and pale lips gave him away.

"That's Aaron!" Barry exclaimed.

Aaron and Beth were in a hallway, walking toward each other. Beth appeared to be deep in concentration, as she didn't glance up when he passed her by. Spinning around, Aaron caught Beth by surprise, squeezing his arm around her neck and cupping a hand over her mouth. He must have known exactly where to press, because she soon went limp, allowing him to toss her over his shoulder and exit via the stairway.

Samantha lifted the receiver off her office telephone. "I'm calling the police."

Barry reached over and depressed the switch hook. "You promised me twenty-four hours."

"That was before I watched the video of a crime being committed in my hallway!"

Barry released the switch hook, circled to the front of the desk, and leaned down. "Please! If you call now, not only could you be sentencing Beth and me to prison for the rest of our lives, but you might also be sentencing Kayleigh to a life of misery. Once the media gets ahold of this, they'll forget today's news conference and focus solely on the abduction. Think about how a kidnapping would reflect on the Blue Loon Village!"

She set down the receiver.

"Thank you," Barry said with relief in his voice. "Jenny will be here in less than four hours, bringing her expertise and um . . . something you don't want to know about. The best thing you can do in the meantime is use that computer of yours to find out all you can about Aaron Anderson."

"Anderson? There must be numerous men in the Twin Cities with the same first and last name."

"Yes, but this one might have been arrested for indecent exposure or public intoxication a little over a year ago. And now that he's homeless, I wouldn't be surprised if Megan filed for divorce."

"Okay. I'll see what I can do."

"While you work on that, I'm going back to my apartment to call homeless shelters. Maybe we'll get lucky, and the recent cold weather will have forced Aaron to spend the night at one. If we find him, we find Beth." He hurried out the door and texted Jenny the latest news as he rode the elevator to the top floor.

CHAPTER 22

Gerontophilia

Aaron unlocked the door to his loft and guided Beth inside. He pointed and ordered, "Sit."

Beth glanced at the cheap metal chair before continuing her gaze to the open package of zip ties on a card table a few feet away. "I have to use the bathroom," she declared.

"Hold it," he demanded.

"I've been holding it all day! Any second I'm gonna have no choice but to let loose and pee on your floor. Then you're either gonna have to clean it up yourself or release my hands so I can do it." She scanned the room. "I don't see a single window. Man, it's really gonna stink in here."

"Fine." He pointed. "The bathroom is that way." He grasped Beth's arm and led her down the hall.

As soon as she stepped inside, Beth said, "I can't pull down my pants with my arms bound like this. You're gonna need to cut the zip tie."

"I'll pull down your pants for you."

"The hell you will!"

"I won't look when I do it."

"Perfect. Then you won't see my knee when it smashes you in the face."

"Hey! I'm the one in control here."

"Yeah, you're a big strong alpha male who's afraid he'll get the shit beat out of him by a little old lady."

"I'm not afraid of you!" he blustered.

"Oh yeah? Prove it!" She turned around to expose her bound arms.

Aaron expelled an exasperated breath. "I need something sharp to cut you loose. Don't move." He stepped out of the bathroom.

Beth decided to obey. . . . For now.

When Aaron returned with a cheap steak knife, he grabbed Beth's arms and yanked them toward his face. She sealed her lips to avoid giving him the pleasure of hearing her cry out. He cut the zip tie and released her arms.

Beth turned to face Aaron. When he didn't move, she flicked a hand at him. "Go on. I'll be out in a moment."

"I honored your request to cut you free. But I'm not leaving you alone in here."

"Oh. My. God," she said with a smirk. "You're a gerontophile!"

"A jerry what?"

"A person who's sexually attracted to people much older than they are."

"I am not!"

She pointed to the cabinet below the sink. "Do you need some lube so you can wank off while you watch me go?"

"No!"

"So you prefer to wank off dry?"

"No!"

"Then why do you need to watch me go?"

"Because you might get away."

"Get away?" She flared out her hands. "There's no window in here. How could I possibly escape?"

"You might find a weapon."

"Do you normally keep weapons in your bathroom?"

"No."

She put her hands on her hips. "Then what's the problem?"

He stared at his feet and mumbled like a child, "Nothing."

"Then get outta here and let me pee in peace."

He backed out.

"And close the door. Otherwise, I'll think you're standing just out of sight—listening and wanking."

He hesitated.

She pumped her fist up and down and glared at him.

He complied.

Beth listened for a moment, then pulled open the cabinet doors and drawers as quietly as possible. There wasn't much: a few rolls of toilet paper, a plunger, a bottle of ibuprofen, shampoo, a nail clipper, a comb, antiperspirant, a bar of soap, toothpaste, and a toothbrush. She slipped the nail clipper into her back pocket and retreated to the toilet. She really did have to pee.

"Hurry up!" Aaron yelled from the hallway.

"I'm almost done, dear," she called back in a singsongy voice.

When Beth opened the door a moment later, Aaron grabbed her arm and escorted her back to the metal chair. "Sit."

She remained standing. "Are you going to punish me now?

Maybe force me to watch while you wank off?"

"I told you. I'm not a jerry . . . whatever. Just sit and put your hands behind your back, so I can secure them."

"So it's bondage of older women that gets you off?"

"No!"

"Then you're into more than just bondage?"

"Shut up! There's nothing sexual about this."

"If that's the case, why do you insist on tying me up?"

"Because you're gonna pay for what you did to me at that school, for forcing me to walk home in shredded underwear, for breaking up my marriage, for causing me to lose my job, and for making me lose my house and live on the streets."

Beth shook her head. "First of all, when I left you at the school, you were still married, you still had your job, and you still had your house. Losing all of that is on you, not me. Second of all, tying me up and punishing me is the very definition of BDSM. You can't expect me to actually believe you aren't gonna wank off after you finish."

Aaron reared back and slapped her across the face with brutal force. She crumpled to the floor. "You fucking bitch!" he roared. "Look what you made me do!"

CHAPTER 23

The Police

When Jenny rang Barry's doorbell he was on the phone, speaking with the last shelter on his list. He opened the door, waved her inside, gestured for her to hang her coat in the closet, and returned to his stool at the kitchen island counter to finish the call.

Hanging up, he said, "You are a sight for sore eyes! Since we've only served homeless people who don't live in shelters, I hadn't fully grasped how many shelters exist in the Twin Cities or how many people use them. According to the homeless shelter directory I found on the internet, there are seventeen metro area shelters serving approximately five thousand people. I called every shelter—some more than once—but could only speak with someone at thirteen of them."

Jenny set her laptop computer on the counter and headed for the refrigerator. Grabbing a soft drink, she circled around to the far side of the counter, plopped onto a stool, and asked, "Did you get any leads?"

"Unfortunately, no. Homeless people come and go and frequently use false names. Complicating matters was that several of the shelters refused to give me any information because of confidentiality issues. And those that did, hadn't seen anyone named Aaron Anderson or anyone fitting his physical description."

"Did you tell them he abducted Beth?"

"No. For the first twenty-four hours, the only people aware of the kidnapping will be you, me, and Samantha."

"What! Why?"

"Because Beth and I would likely go to prison for our vigilantism that started it all. Also, if the media learned that Beth was abducted from the Blue Loon Village, her story would overwhelm any stories about the news conference we held here this morning to help Kayleigh."

"Did Samantha make you agree to the twenty-four-hour deadline?"

"Uh-huh."

"Good. Because if she hadn't, I would've. Is there anything else I should know?"

"Other than what I included in the text I sent you, I don't think so. But that reminds me. . . ." He scooped up his phone from the counter and tapped in a text. Setting the phone back down, he continued, "Samantha is also searching for information on Aaron. I just asked her to send me what she's found so far."

Jenny opened her computer and logged on to Barry's internet service. Neither said a word while she tapped the keys, searching for clues, and he heated some milk for hot chocolate. When Barry's phone vibrated to announce a return text from Samantha, he forwarded it to Jenny.

She reviewed the text and said, "I'm impressed. Samantha did some first-rate digging and found Aaron's divorce attorney, Gunther Lee. She says Gunther tried to reach Aaron on her behalf by dialing the only phone number he had on file. Unfortunately, that call reached the warehouse where Aaron worked. No one there had seen him for several days or knew where he lived. Gunther also suggested that if Aaron was in trouble, he could find out the name of the bank where Aaron deposited his settlement check and ask them if they had additional contact information. Such an inquiry would require a court order, however."

"I'm impressed too. Especially since it sounds as if Samantha kept my reasons for wanting to find Aaron confidential."

"Beyond the calls you made, and the research Samantha did, the only other thing I can think of is to contact Aaron's ex-wife."

"That's probably how Samantha reached Aaron's attorney. Let me check." He picked up his phone, put it on the speaker setting, and dialed Samantha's cell.

"Did you get my text?" she asked immediately.

"Yes. And Jenny and I are both impressed that you found Aaron's divorce attorney. How'd you manage that?"

"I walked over to Memory Care to visit Nadine and caught her during one of her good days. She hadn't spoken with Aaron since her granddaughter, Megan, filed for divorce and suggested contacting Megan at her new phone number. I did that, and she, likewise, hadn't spoken with Aaron. Instead, she gave me the number for his attorney, saying that was the only way she knew how to reach him."

"Well, good job."

"Are you two making any additional progress?"

"I've hit a dead end, but Jenny is just getting started."

"Keep me informed."

"I will." He hung up.

Jenny looked at Barry and shook her head. "If homeless shelters and Aaron's attorney and ex-wife can't lead us to Beth, I don't know who can."

"We could take Gunther up on his offer to contact the bank."

"Yeah, but no judge is gonna hand over a court order without police involvement."

"True."

"Let me concentrate for a bit." Jenny stared at her computer screen, tapped some keys, stared some more, and repeated the cycle numerous times. Finally, she pushed her laptop aside and said, "You probably thought I was some computer genius who could solve a kidnapping via the internet. I'm not that good. And frankly, in this situation, I don't think anyone is that good. We can't wait twenty-four hours. We need to call the police. Now!"

Barry shifted on his stool and let out a loud sigh before saying, "Fine."

Jenny put a hand on Barry's arm. "We'll ask the police to be discrete. And if you end up in prison after all of this, I promise to visit you at least once a month."

"I might be overreacting about the prison thing."

"Might?" Jenny snarked.

"Okay. . . . Probably. If the police find Beth, and Aaron doesn't get himself killed before he's arrested, any claims he has about what Beth and I did to him will be suspect. But my second reason for staying quiet still stands. We can't overwhelm the news conference for Kayleigh with another story originating from the Blue Loon Village that's more sensational."

"Then let me be the primary police contact. All my years as a cop's wife have taught me how to speak their language. But first, let's review everything—even things you've told me before. We must avoid conflicting stories."

While Barry was never much for details, he concentrated on recalling his and Beth's history with Aaron as accurately as possible. When he finished, he pushed away from the counter and said, "While you call the cops, I'm going downstairs to find Samantha. She needs to hear what I've just told you."

"See you soon," she replied.

CHAPTER 24

The Warehouse District

Upon selecting the director's office for their meeting location, Barry, Jenny, and Samantha spoke with a uniformed police officer. That interview was cut short when John Sorenson, a handsome white-shirted detective, showed up to send the police officer away and make them start all over again. Barry did his best to hide his irritation about the inefficiency of having to repeat himself. Samantha, on the other hand, reveled in the detective's attention, becoming what Barry would later describe as "flirty as fuck."

The interview with Detective Sorenson concluded well after the Blue Loon Village had gone quiet for the evening. As Barry waited on the first floor for the elevator to arrive, he said to Jenny, "If you're ready to call it a night, you're welcome to go directly to Beth's apartment. I've already put fresh sheets on the bed."

"You know how to make a bed?"

"Of course! Now, folding a fitted sheet is a whole nother matter."

"All joking aside, how are you holding up?"

"Each passing minute makes me more terrified for Beth. I've seen what Aaron is capable of."

"I'm terrified for her, too. And even though Detective Sorenson is now on the case, I doubt I could fall asleep at the moment."

"I don't know what else we can do tonight. But if you wanna keep working on this, I'll do the same."

"One thing we learned today is that Aaron works at a warehouse. Doesn't Minneapolis have something called the Warehouse District?"

"Yeah. It's downtown, near the First Avenue nightclub and the Minnesota Twins' baseball stadium."

Stepping into the elevator, Jenny said, "How about if I make us two coffees to go and we spend a few hours cruising the Warehouse District? It probably won't get us anywhere, but it'll beat tossing and turning in bed."

"Sure," Barry said, pushing the fourth-floor button. "We'll take my Mustang."

"That goes without saying. Can I drive? I know your history of unintended naps."

"Since I know Minneapolis better than you do, it'll be more efficient if I drive. But if you catch me yawning, you have my permission to relegate me to the passenger seat."

* * *

Upon reaching Hennepin Avenue, Barry drove a grid, pointing out well-known landmarks along the way. While nightclubs such as The Fine Line and First Avenue were still lit up and busy, most of the old brick warehouses and storefronts were dark and quiet. When the grid took them beyond the major streets, Barry pulled over, retrieved two high-powered flashlights from the vigilante tool kit he'd tossed into the back seat, and handed one to Jenny.

"Thanks. Though I don't know what good it will do. We have no idea what Aaron is driving, and even if he has accommodations around here, we're not gonna be able to see inside."

"As you said, it beats tossing and turning in bed." He steered away from the curb and continued down the street.

Several blocks later, Jenny pointed and suggested, "Let's drive through the alleys instead."

Barry offered a slight nod and turned into a dark alley. They both knew their chances of finding Beth hadn't increased, yet somehow driving behind the buildings felt more promising. With narrow passageways between cars and dumpsters jammed wherever they could fit, and the occasional dimly lit window several stories up, the alleys felt creepy. Surely, any place Aaron took Beth would be creepy.

When Barry finally yawned, Jenny unbuckled her seatbelt with as much gusto as she could muster. Feeling too exhausted to object, Barry shifted the Mustang into park and switched seats with her. Using his flashlight to scan the alleys from the passenger seat would put less strain on his arthritic neck anyway.

Jenny continued driving the grid until they'd squeezed through nearly every alley and hit nearly every dead end in what could reasonably be considered the Warehouse District.

Barry flicked off his flashlight, leaned back, and closed his eyes.

"It's almost one," said Jenny. "We should probably head back to the Blue Loon Village."

"Yeah, okay," he mumbled. "Do you know the way?"

"I think I can figure it out."

Barry was snoring by the time the Mustang reached I-35.

Jenny glanced across her shoulder, envious of her friend's ability to fall asleep so easily. She considered turning on the radio before opting to listen to the rumble of the engine. After all, the Blue Loon Village wasn't too far away. She depressed the accelerator, hoping to feel the rush that came with all that power.

Flashing lights ahead shortened her rush. The bars were closing, and the police were on the prowl for drunk drivers. She tapped the brakes, returning to a speed that would keep her out of trouble.

Barry's cell phone chimed, jerking him awake.

"Do you want me to get that for you?" Jenny asked.

Extending his arm toward the center console, he replied, "No, I've got it." He picked up his phone and glanced at the screen. "I don't recognize the number. Goddamn telemarketers never leave me alone. They keep calling later and later." He pushed the green icon and blurted, "I don't need a Medicare supplement! Quit calling me!"

"How 'bout a big wet kiss?"

CHAPTER 25

The Gay 90s

"Beth?" Barry hit the speakerphone icon. "Come get me."

"Where are you?"

"At the front entrance of the Gay 90s. Do you know where that is?"

"I do," said Jenny. She sped up, looking for one of the connecting roads between the north and south sides of the freeway that only cops and highway workers are supposed to use.

"What a relief to hear your voice!" Barry exclaimed. "Are you okay?"

"Considering all that has happened, yes."

"What are you doing at a gay bar?" Barry asked.

"Aaron has a loft above a warehouse near here. I was locked in his trunk when he drove me there, so I didn't know where I was. When I escaped, I picked a direction and ran until I spotted a sign for Hennepin Avenue. From there, I oriented myself and hurried to the first place I knew there'd be a crowd of people. A nice, ah . . . woman, taller than you and just as pretty as Jenny, lent me her phone."

"How'd you escape?" Barry asked.

"I'll tell you when you get here."

"We'll be there in ten minutes," Jenny proclaimed.

Beth's voice grew skeptical. "Even the Mustang isn't fast enough to get you here that quickly."

"Yes, it is," Jenny insisted. "The downtown exit is just ahead."

"How'd you—"

"I'll tell you when we get there," Jenny said.

* * *

When the Mustang pulled up in front of the Gay 90s, four muscular drag queens wearing tight dresses, spiked heels, and impeccable makeup were guarding Beth. She bolted for the car, only to be stopped by an outstretched arm.

"Just a moment, ma'am," said one of the queens. "We need to make sure it's safe."

Another queen flashed a palm as he approached the Mustang, then motioned for Barry to lower his window. Leaning down, he asked, "Your name, sir?"

"Barry."

"And yours, ma'am?"

"Jenny."

"Please open the door so I can check the back seat."

Barry stepped onto the sidewalk, leaving the door open for inspection. Once the queen turned and nodded to the others, Beth broke away, greeting Barry in a tight embrace before switching to Jenny, who had raced around the front of the car.

"I've got so much to tell both of you!" Beth exclaimed. "But first I need a drink."

"Here?" Barry asked.

Beth let go of Jenny. "It's tempting. Are the police looking for me?"

"You're one of their top priorities," said Barry. "Security cameras in the hallway caught the whole thing."

"Then I'm guessing that partying at the Gay 90s with the two of you and my new drag queen friends before informing the cops would be frowned upon."

"I'll call them to let them know we're on the way to the Blue Loon Village. I'm sure they'll wanna speak with you in-person."

"We'll drink at the apartment, then."

Barry returned to the car and grabbed his smartphone before squeezing into the back seat; Jenny returned to the driver's seat; and Beth turned to the drag queens and blew them a kiss. "Thank you all for everything!" she shouted.

The queens waved and blew kisses of their own.

Beth dropped into the passenger seat and proclaimed, "You won't believe—" She stopped, realizing that Barry was already talking to the police.

Because he wasn't using the speakerphone, all she heard was his side of the conversation. "Uh-huh. . . . Beth Potter. . . . She escaped. . . . Yes. . . . She's fine. . . . Would you like to speak with her? . . . I'll hold. . . . The Blue Loon Village. . . . Apartment 456. . . . Not yet. . . . We're headed there now. . . . Fifteen minutes. . . . We'll stay up until he arrives. . . . Thank you."

The Mustang had already merged onto I-35 by the time Barry hung up.

Jenny shot Beth an inquiring look. "Well?"

"You won't believe," she repeated before glancing at the

dashboard clock and hesitating. "You know what? Since I'm gonna be telling my story to the police in a few minutes, I'll just wait and tell all of you at the same time."

"The hell you will!" Jenny blurted.

"We wanna hear it now," Barry whined.

"How 'bout if I give you the short version and save the details for later?"

"We can live with that," said Barry.

"Diarrhea," Beth said.

"That's it?" Jenny asked. "You've gotta give us more than that."

"Have you ever noticed that kidnappers in movies and TV shows never have to go to the bathroom? Well, abducting someone in real life is not only stressful for the abductee, but it's also stressful for the abductor. Either that or Aaron ate way too much chili for lunch. Whatever it was that gave him the trots, they hit him hard shortly after he brought me to his loft, forced me to sit in a chair, and bound my wrists with a zip tie. Each time he raced to the toilet, I worked on the zip tie with a nail clipper I'd stolen from a drawer and hidden in my back pocket."

"Wait a minute," said Barry. "Back up a bit and tell us how you got there."

"All I know is that I awoke in the trunk of Aaron's car. He left me there for hours until it got dark enough for him to walk me up the stairs to his loft. Perhaps I should call it a *lair* instead of a loft. It was just a big open room with ratty furniture and a bathroom without a shower or a tub. There wasn't even a kitchen, only a mini-fridge and a plug-in burner."

Barry leaned forward. "I learned a bit about places like that from a musician I got to know when I was still working in radio. The owners of some buildings in the Warehouse District have renovated their upper levels into trendy loft apartments; others have done less and turned those spaces into studios for musicians, artists, and photographers. One of those studios would be ideal for someone in need of an inexpensive place to stay and a private place for revenge. Do you remember where it's located?"

"I raced out of there while Aaron was on the toilet and didn't look back. If I look at a map or Google Street View, I might be able to narrow it down for the cops. For now, all I can say is that it's within four blocks of the Gay 90s."

Upon arriving at the Blue Loon Village, the three friends crossed the parking lot and proceeded to the elevator. It was under the bright elevator lights that Barry noticed the bruise on Beth's jaw and exclaimed, "Oh, my God! What happened?"

"Aaron got rough with me a few times. It would've been worse if it weren't for his runs to the bathroom and me keeping him talking."

"We should've dumped that fucker in the Mississippi River a year ago, when we had the chance."

"And be just as bad as him?" The elevator doors opened. "It may take the cops a few days to find Aaron, but when they do, he'll be spending a long time in jail."

Barry followed the women into the hallway and said to Beth, "Let's hope he doesn't take us to jail with him."

Jenny looked at the ceiling and said, "Oh jeez, here we go again."

Beth added, "We're not going to jail for frightening Aaron and sending him on an intoxicated semi-naked walk." She gave Barry a slight bump as he turned to open his door. "I know incessant worrying is your job in our relationship, but in this instance you're just too damn paranoid. No cop is going to listen to Aaron. And even if one did, his story won't amount to anything unless you or I confirm it with a confession."

Once inside the apartment, Barry walked straight to the bathroom, Jenny dropped the car keys on the counter, and Beth opened a bottle of wine. When Barry returned, Beth poured the wine, and they all moved to the living room, where the women settled onto the couch and Barry sank into his recliner.

Barry took a sip before complaining, "Now, if the cops would just show up, we could get this over with and go to sleep."

The doorbell rang.

Jenny giggled. "Barry Swanson and his amazing curmudgeonly powers!"

* * *

If Detective Sorenson appeared as if he had just rolled out of bed, it was because that was exactly what had happened. A kidnapping case involving a celebrity was too high-profile to trust the nearest cop in a squad car to handle.

The interview went on into the night, until Barry grumbled to the detective, "How many different ways does Beth need to tell you the same thing?"

"He's just trying to be thorough," admonished Samantha, who had joined the interview after driving over from her nearby house.

"That's okay," the detective replied. "I don't have any more questions at this time, and I have all of your phone numbers if something comes up."

"Are you going to supply the Blue Loon Village with extra security?" Samantha asked.

"I don't think that'll be necessary," he said, pocketing his notepad. "Mr. Anderson will correctly assume that every police officer in the greater Twin Cities area is looking for him. Returning here would be too big of a risk for him to take. Instead, I recommend that you ask your residents to keep their doors locked and only walk the halls or ride the elevator in groups of two or more. I'll let you know the moment we capture Mr. Anderson."

Samantha stood. "Thank you, Detective Sorenson. I'll issue a memo to my staff and residents first thing in the morning. In the meantime, would you mind walking me to my car?"

"It would be my pleasure, ma'am."

CHAPTER 26

Aaron's Story, Part 8

Aaron seethed. Whether he was seething because he'd just lost his second battle to the old woman or because he was paying the price for stupidly finishing off some dodgy leftovers he'd forgotten to stuff into his mini-fridge, even he didn't know. Being alone with his temper felt much worse than being with someone he could release it upon.

Oh, how he wished Beth's neck was between his hands—or even Megan's. He didn't care which. Both women had conspired to ruin his life, and both deserved his retribution. Since neither was reachable at the moment, he considered his own role in falling from a gainfully employed alpha family man, to living on the streets, to his current state of looking at the open door of his loft with his pants around his ankles.

"How could you be so stupid!" he shouted at himself. A bolt of light shot through his brain as he slammed his head against the bathroom doorframe. Staggering for a moment, he craned back his neck for a second blow, paused, and, upon realizing that knocking himself out would only compound his stupidity, reached down to pull up his pants.

Having accomplished that, he dashed out of the loft, descended the stairs, and hurried into the alley, where he looked both ways. When he was still on the toilet, he had heard a click and foolishly convinced himself that it was just one of the normal noises in the building. After all, if he had accepted the reality that Beth was escaping, he would've had to leap off the toilet and risk spraying the remaining contents of his bowels into his underwear, or on the bathroom floor, or in the hallway, as he gave chase. And for an alpha male like him, the embarrassment of chasing down an old woman and forcing her back into the loft, where she'd see and smell the foul biological mess he created, would be worse than her getting away.

With no sign of Beth in either direction, Aaron accepted that searching for her in the dark city would be futile. Right now, he needed to grab his valuables and abandon the loft before the police arrived. If there was one positive to his current situation, it was that a year of homelessness had taught him how to disappear. Later, he could make another run at Beth, or, if he so desired, switch to the old man she hung out with.

"If at first you don't succeed, try, try again," he whispered to himself.

CHAPTER 27

Another News Conference

After Samantha and Detective Sorenson departed, Jenny decided not to move downstairs to Beth's apartment. Instead, Barry set her up on the couch with fresh sheets, a blanket, and a pillow. Then Beth, as she often did, shared the bed with Barry. Until Aaron was apprehended, following the detective's advice of staying in groups of two or more was the prudent thing to do.

Despite everything that had happened, Barry fell asleep after a few minutes. Beth, on the other hand, struggled to turn off her brain. Even though she had refused the detective's offer to set her up with a counselor, the trauma of her abduction wasn't going to disappear instantly now that she'd escaped. More than once, she had to extract herself from Barry's arms because the contact brought on the panicky feeling of being restrained in Aaron's trunk. That Aaron was able to steal the pleasure of physical contact with her lover infuriated her—even if that theft was only temporary.

Come morning, the crackle of eggs and the aroma of coffee enticed the women from their blanket cocoons. "I thought we'd all be more comfortable eating here instead of the cafeteria," Barry declared a bit too brightly.

Jenny squinted as she looked across the counter. "The last time I opened your refrigerator, it was almost empty. Did you go to the grocery store this morning?"

He smiled. "I have connections in the cafeteria."

"You've never cooked for me before. Is it safe?"

"I used to cook for my wife all the time."

Jenny's eyelids widened a notch. "I don't think you meant to give me that opening."

Barry glanced down to flip the eggs. "I suppose not."

Beth eased onto a stool at the counter and let out an exaggerated yawn.

"That's quite a yawn," said Barry. "Did you get any sleep last night?"

"Maybe an hour or two. It took me forever to push aside everything that happened with Aaron; then I started thinking about Kayleigh. How'd yesterday's news conference go?"

"I was only there at the beginning," Barry said as he extracted three plates from the cupboard. "But it must've gone well, because I saw a story about it on the front page of this morning's newspaper when I walked downstairs to acquire the eggs for our breakfast. Emma was nervous about taking over the news conference when I left to search for you, but I knew she'd do fine. Who better than a mother to tell her daughter's tragic story?"

Jenny settled in next to Beth. "To make sure your abduction wouldn't overwhelm Kayleigh's story, Barry insisted that no one call the cops until we'd spent twenty-four hours trying to find you on our own. Later, he realized we were utter failures at being detectives and relented to calling them much sooner."

Barry scowled at Jenny. "Did you have to tell her that?"

"Oh, please. She would've found out eventually. Probably when you blurted it out by accident."

"It's okay," Beth said, pouring herself a glass of orange juice. "If I had a choice, I would've wanted you guys to delay too. If Kayleigh gets her operation, she'll have many more joyful years ahead of her than I will."

After sliding loaded plates across the counter, Barry took a plate for himself and sat opposite the women. Looking at Beth, he said, "Because we didn't immediately call the police, and your escape happened so late last night, the print and broadcast news services are probably just learning about what happened. That'll give Kayleigh's story longer to take hold." He pointed to the hallway leading to the bedroom. "I rescued your purse from the lectern and put it on my dresser. I also braved reaching inside it to turn off your phone. As we speak, the media is probably filling up your voicemail with messages."

"Thanks. I saw it. I'll deal with the messages after breakfast and a shower."

* * *

Beth was on the couch next to Barry, listening to what seemed like an endless string of voicemails, when she threw up her hands and announced, "We need to schedule another news conference!"

Barry leaned forward to grab his phone off the coffee table. Turning it on, he said, "When I went downstairs this morning, I noticed the stage was still set up. I'll send a text to Samantha."

When Barry's phone pinged with Samantha's response, he read the text out loud. "Great idea! I've been getting calls too but didn't want to bother you until I was sure you were awake. The media will have to get by without the finger food table, however. What time?"

"Tell her two o'clock," Beth said.

Barry typed a response and set his phone back on the table. He thought for a moment, picked up his phone again, and typed a second text. This time to John Sorenson.

* * *

Detective Sorenson opened the news conference by showing the security camera video of Beth's abduction and a mug shot of Aaron Anderson from the previous year. After that, he discussed the manhunt that was under way and took a few questions.

When the detective finished, Beth replaced him behind the lectern, with Jenny on one side and Barry on the other. She didn't have a speech planned and instead gave the reporters her view of the previous day's events and opened the floor to questions.

"Ms. Potter!" voices shouted in unison.

Beth pointed to a young woman bundled in a heavy sweater.

"What was it like being locked in the trunk of a car for so long?"

"Dark and cold. I wish I'd been wearing your sweater."

A pudgy man with black-rimmed glasses raised his hand.

Beth pointed. "Go ahead."

"Most of us remember the three of you becoming celebrities after the creative use of a can of SPAM to take down a mass shooter at a nightclub. Hearing now how you escaped your captor after he became disabled by a bout of explosive diarrhea, I have to ask—was that another creative use of SPAM?"

Half the reporters chuckled. The rest cringed.

"That would be creative, dear. But it's never a good idea to risk insulting the SPAM Gods. If I'd used SPAM to help me escape, it would've been because my captor was too enamored with the delicious meat to abandon it and give chase."

More chuckles.

A gaunt, gray-haired man raised a hand. When Beth pointed to him, he said, "I have a two-part question. First, I'd like to know if you'd previously met Aaron Anderson. Second, I wonder if you know why he abducted you?"

Beth leaned forward, with each hand grasping a side of the lectern. She thought for a moment before deciding to spice up her answer. If what she was about to say helped Kayleigh get the necessary medical treatment, she'd gladly bend the truth into politician territory. "Mr. Anderson has a violent history, and I witnessed that history a year ago when he threatened to beat Barry with a tire iron. I didn't see Mr. Anderson again until last month, when I was delivering food to the homeless and found him living in a tent. As for why he abducted me, don't you think it's a strange coincidence that Mr. Anderson was suddenly no longer homeless and able to grab me just before I was to lead yesterday's news conference? That news conference, as you'll remember, was to discuss Carephyx Healthnyt's continued refusal to cover a critical surgical procedure for fifteen-year-old Kayleigh Clark."

A man with a neatly trimmed red beard raised his hand.

Beth pointed. "Yes."

"Are you accusing Edward Thomas, the CEO of Carephyx

Healthnyt, of arranging your abduction?"

Beth shook her head. "I'm merely suggesting that it's one of many possibilities and will leave it up to the police to solve the case." She paused to scan the room. "After all that has happened, the big original question remains. Why is Mr. Thomas still putting corporate profits ahead of a fifteen-year-old girl's life?"

When no one shouted an answer, Beth said, "Next question."

A middle-aged reporter with a comb-over raised his hand. "Has being abducted by a homeless man changed your opinion of helping the homeless?"

Beth tilted her head as she replied, "Why would I allow one person to do that? The vast majority of homeless people I've met over the past year have been polite and appreciative. You'll find criminals among people in all walks of life, from preachers to politicians. The homeless are no different."

She continued answering questions as Jenny and Barry stood by her side, wondering why they had agreed to participate and if anyone would notice if they slowly shuffled offstage.

When a round-faced man finally directed a question to Barry, it caught him off-guard. "Mr. Swanson. What's next for the Silver Squad?"

Barry sucked in his lips before replying, "After our well-publicized events of a year ago, I think we started to believe our own hype—almost like we were superheroes or something. But the truth is that we were mostly lucky. The same goes for Beth escaping her abductor. I mean, come on, which took more luck—me hitting a mass shooter in the temple with a can of SPAM or Beth's kidnapper coming down with a case of explosive diarrhea? Since it's obvious that the powers that be at Carephyx Healthnyt only have empathy for their stockholders, not their policyholders, all I want now is for our luck to rub off on young Kayleigh."

He considered his next words before continuing. "When I met Kayleigh, my first thought was that any CEO unethical enough to deny her healthcare deserved to be shot down in cold blood, just like what happened to that insurance company CEO in New York City. But what good would that do? Some other greedy bastard would simply take his place. Instead, do you know what works? Boycotts. So, I hope all of you will appreciate the three-fer we're giving you today. Instead of leaving this news conference with just one story, you'll leave it with three: the story of Beth escaping her abductor and the Silver Squad calling for a nationwide boycott of Carephyx Healthnyt. Thank you."

Barry stepped back from the lectern, apparently oblivious to the reporters' confused expressions. His lips barely moved as he counted to himself, "Five, four, three, two, one."

A reporter with long dreadlocks raised her hand and shouted, "Mr. Swanson. That's only two stories. What's the third?"

He returned to the lectern and turned sideways as he spoke into the microphone. "Beth Potter. Will you marry me?"

CHAPTER 28

The Phone Call

Beth didn't give Barry an answer onstage. Instead, she turned his proposal into a joke. "Focus Barry! Let's see if the press can cover two stories at once, not three." She swept a hand from one side of the room to the other as she said, "I'll let you all know my answer once Carephyx Healthnyt demonstrates that the first part of their name is pronounced Carefix not Carefucks and approves the surgery for Kayleigh."

At the conclusion of their news conference, the three friends walked silently to the elevator. As they stepped inside, Jenny moved as far away from Barry and Beth as the elevator walls would allow.

Beth, on the other hand, stood face-to-face with Barry and shouted, "What the hell was that! We have a good thing going between us. Why would you want to ruin it with a proposal in front of a bunch of reporters?"

"I'm sorry. I hadn't put any thought into proposing since we discussed the pluses and minuses of marriage on our way home from Des Moines. It just kinda came out."

"What! You asked me to marry you without putting any thought into it?"

"That's not what I meant. I've actually thought a lot about us getting married. I just never thought about how I would propose to you once I talked myself into it."

"You had to talk yourself into proposing to me?"

Barry covered his face.

Beth gave Jenny a quick wink.

Jenny bit her lip.

When the elevator doors opened, Beth charged into the hallway, leaving Barry to stick out his arm to prevent the doors from closing. Jenny followed, whispering, "She's just giving you shit," as she passed him by.

"I know," he whispered back.

* * *

"Do you think my boycott idea will work?" Barry asked from his recliner once everyone had settled back into his apartment.

Beth replied from the couch, "The threat of a boycott might. As for an actual boycott, no."

"Why?"

"Because many people have Carephyx Healthnyt through their employers and therefore have no choice of providers. Others will think switching is too much trouble. One thing we have in our favor, however, is that we're near the end of the year. Carephyx customers who take advantage of the Health Insurance Marketplace or Medicare Advantage plans can easily switch their providers for the coming year."

Jenny carried a soft drink in from the kitchen and plopped

down next to Beth. "If nothing else, I'm confident we've inspired a vigorous debate among the top executives at Carephyx Healthnyt. Some won't want to give in, because they'd be setting a precedent. Others will prefer to relent, so we will go away."

The three friends continued chatting through dinner and into the night. When they picked up again on the following day, Jenny reported to Barry and Beth that she'd modified their social media videos to encourage a nationwide boycott of Carephyx Healthnyt.

By late afternoon, everyone was confident they'd done all they could to help Kayleigh for the time being, and their conversations drifted onto other subjects, such as whether Gertrude's terrarium was emitting an odor and whether Detective Sorenson would respond to Samantha's flirting and ask her out on a date.

Knowing that Jenny was planning to return to Des Moines in the morning, Barry mixed a round of farewell drinks and joined the women at the counter. Spying his smartphone charging near the wall, he reached over to disconnect it. He had read that overcharging would shorten the battery's life and didn't want to be one of those wasteful people who had to update their phone every year or so.

Upon disconnecting his phone from the USB cord, he slid his thumb toward the side button to turn it off for the evening. The phone chimed before he could push it. Looking at the screen, he recognized his son's cell phone number and tapped the icon to answer. "Hi Harry! What's up?"

"I met someone at the Gay 90s."

"That's not supri— Wait, say that again."

"I met someone at the Gay 90s."

Barry tapped the speakerphone icon and set his phone on the counter. "You don't sound like Harry. Who is this?"

"I think you know who I am."

"Let me speak to Harry!"

"I have him in a safe place."

"How do I know you're telling the truth?"

"You obviously recognized the number I called from."

"So?"

"That's all the proof you need."

"What do you want?"

"To win the war."

"War? What war?"

"You and your old lady won our first two battles. Purely by luck, I might add. Now I'm going to win the war."

"How are you gonna do that?"

"Aren't you curious about how I captured your son?"

Barry balled his fists. "He'll have plenty of time to tell me all about it after I beat you to a pulp!"

"When word got out that your old lady fled to the Gay 90s after she escaped, I was curious why she picked that establishment. Did she know someone there? And if so, what information did she share about me? I started asking around and learned that your son was in the crowd outside when you arrived in your Mustang."

"So?"

"As soon as he saw you, he disappeared inside."

"Why would he do that? I've known he's gay for years."

"But did you know he's a popular drag queen—a regular celebrity at the Gay 90s?"

"I didn't know that. But he's my son, and though we don't talk as often as we should, nothing he could do would change the love I feel for him."

"Apparently, he believes differently. Though he's not as shy around people he believes to be his fans."

Barry sighed.

Aaron continued. "Here's what's gonna happen. I'm going to give you until ten tomorrow morning to come up with fifteen thousand dollars in unmarked bills in an assortment of denominations. Then I'm gonna send you a text with additional instructions."

"Okay, I can do that."

"I'm not finished. You must bring your old lady and that blonde chick with you. If you call the cops or bring weapons, I will disappear, and you'll never find Harry in time."

"What do you mean, 'in time'?"

"He'll be zip-tied, much like your old lady zip-tied me a year ago. Only tomorrow the weather is gonna be much colder."

"I'll do what you ask, but I can't bring the girl."

"Then your son will freeze."

"You don't understand!" Barry screamed. "I'd bring her if I could, but she left for the airport a few hours ago. She's flying to San Diego to visit her stepsister. There's no way she could return in time. I might be able to get her back by tomorrow evening, but I doubt you want to risk such a delay. Besides, your dispute is with Beth and me, not her."

Silence.

"Aaron, are you there?"

"Yes," he hissed. "I'm thinking. . . . Okay. You can come without the blonde chick. But you must pay a penalty."

"What sort of penalty?"

"Now you have to bring me twenty thousand dollars."

"Twenty thousand dollars! I'm a retiree on Social Security.

Do you think I'm made of money?"

"Do you think I give a shit? Steal the money if you have to. Otherwise, you'll never see your son alive again."

"Fine," Barry huffed.

"One last thing."

"What?"

"You must drive your Mustang—no other car is acceptable—and make sure it has a full tank of gas." He hung up.

Jenny waited to make sure the call disconnected, then she looked at Barry and proclaimed, "There's no way you're sending me home!"

"I knew you'd object. Aaron's last words suggest what he has in mind for us tomorrow. He's going to send us on some sort of goose chase while he observes to make sure we're alone and the cops aren't following us. Since you're not going home, I recommend that you and your Glock make yourselves comfortable in my trunk. You'll need warm clothes, something to drink, a blanket, and plenty of pillows. In the meantime, let's head out to the parking lot. I'll show you where the trunk release handle is."

CHAPTER 29

The Twin Cities Tour

After a light breakfast, which included less coffee and juice than usual, Barry and Beth walked out the front door of the Blue Loon Village, crossed the parking lot to the Mustang, and slid into their respective seats.

Barry started the engine, turned to Beth, and said, "Let's hope the snowstorm predicted for today arrives late."

Aware that Aaron could be watching, Barry backed out of his space, circled around to the rear of the building, and popped the trunk. Jenny, dressed in a winter coat and carrying pillows and other supplies, hurried through the double doors, climbed into the trunk, and pulled the lid shut.

She took a moment to arrange her pillows and blanket into a nest before tapping the icon on her phone to call Beth. "I'm ready."

Beth looked at Barry and relayed, "She's ready."

He shifted the car into gear, returned to the front of the building, and continued to the main road.

Since the nearest branch of Beth's bank was closer than Barry's bank was, and she had the necessary funds in her account, they stopped there first. Unfortunately, leaving a bank with twenty thousand dollars in cash isn't a quick or easy task. In this instance, the bank couldn't give Beth the full amount without ordering a portion of it delivered from the next closest branch. Rather than wait or attempt to speed up the process by divulging the reason for her withdrawal, she took what she could get without a delay, and they moved on to Barry's bank a mile away. Even then, they ended up being two thousand dollars short.

Before departing the bank parking lot, Barry dropped the bills into a small duffel bag. "I thought all this money would take up more space." He ruffled them up a bit. "I don't plan on giving this to Aaron unless we absolutely have to. And even if we do hand it over, I doubt he'll stick around to count it."

Beth ripped a strip from a paper bag, wrote *IOU $2,000* on it, scribbled her signature, and handed it to Barry. "Hide this between some bills near the bottom. Being dishonest about our transaction is bad luck."

Barry wasn't in a laughing mood. He'd chuckle about the IOU later, if he got his son back.

Beth raised her smartphone to her face. "It's a minute before ten. How are you doing back there?"

"Okay, I guess," said Jenny. "I've finally overcome the waves of claustrophobia I was feeling. All I ask is that you try to warn me if Barry has to make any sudden maneuvers, so I can brace myself."

Barry's phone pinged. He tapped the screen and read the text aloud. "You have fifteen minutes to reach the Gay 90s."

"Now might be a good time to brace yourself," Beth said

to Jenny before tossing the duffel with the money into the back seat.

The morning traffic had cleared somewhat. Still, reaching their destination on Hennepin Avenue required aggressive driving, which included gunning the Mustang out of the parking lot, weaving through traffic, and ignoring stop lights.

A text arrived three minutes after they pulled up in front of the Gay 90s: *Step out of the car, leave the door open, take photographs of the front and back seats and the Gay 90s marquee. You have 1 minute to send them to me.*

Barry did as he was instructed.

Another text arrived: *Proceed west to I-94, go north, be in the far-right lane as you pass under Broadway Avenue, pull over and wait. You have 12 minutes.*

Barry handed his phone to Beth, squealed the tires around the next corner, and sped toward the I-94 entrance ramp.

"Holy shit!" Jenny shouted via the open connection between her and Beth's cell phones. "A little warning, please!"

Now holding two phones, Beth switched hers to speakerphone and set it on the center console. "Sorry! Aaron gave us twelve minutes to take I-94 north and pass under Broadway Avenue. It's not too far."

They reached their destination with time to spare. From their position parked along the side of the freeway, Barry and Beth looked in all directions expecting to see Aaron approach the car.

A text arrived five minutes later. Beth read it aloud, "Continue north. Take MN-252, cross Brookdale Drive, pull over and wait. You have eight minutes."

Barry accelerated back onto the freeway.

They reached their destination in plenty of time.

As they waited, Beth said, "So far this has been too easy. I wonder what he's up to?"

Jenny's voice rose from Beth's phone. "Since I have nothing better to do, I brought up a map of Twin Cities traffic cameras. Each destination so far has been near a camera that's streaming a live feed. Aaron must be watching that feed to make sure we don't have any cops following us. It's also why he insisted we travel in Barry's easy-to-recognize Mustang. My guess is that our Twin Cities tour will continue until he's positive we're alone. Then the real fun will begin."

The next text arrived. Beth read it so all could hear, "Drive south to US-169, exit at Marystown Road, backtrack to Shakopee High School, enter the parking lot from 17th Ave East, wait there. You have twenty-eight minutes."

This journey would be trickier, because they had already crossed the Brookdale Drive exit. Barry accelerated north. When he found a spot where he could U-turn, he swung the Mustang around, took MN 252 south, merged onto MN-100, and increased his speed.

Jenny called out, "My map program lists our driving time at thirty-three minutes. I'm now switching back to the traffic cameras. I'll do my best to stay at least one camera ahead of you, so I can warn you of any congestion."

Barry sped up some more. "This is gonna get ridiculous. I understand Aaron's desire to make sure no cops are accompanying us, but if he makes me drive too fast, cops are exactly what we're gonna attract."

Beth put a hand on Barry's arm. "Just concentrate on the road, dear. I'll watch for speed traps."

Weaving one way and then the other, the Mustang zoomed past cars, pickups, and semitrucks.

Next—a long section of open road. Barry punched the accelerator.

Next—a wall of vehicles. Barry yelled, "Hold on, Jenny!" as he stomped on the brakes.

With tires squealing, he swerved onto the shoulder and returned his foot to the accelerator.

"We should be hitting a traffic jam just about now," Jenny said with a lilt.

Ignoring Jenny's comment, Barry locked his eyes on the shoulder and hoped that any cops ahead would be blocked on the opposite side of the traffic.

"Sorry! Sorry! Sorry!" he apologized to drivers he knew couldn't hear him, but he assumed were flipping him the bird.

As they reached the front edge of the traffic jam, Barry was relieved to see the culprit was only an old mattress that had fallen off a truck, not a pack of highway patrol cars deliberately driving slowly. He veered onto an uncongested lane and continued speeding south toward Shakopee.

At the same time Barry was maneuvering around the traffic jam, Beth was entering their destination into the dashboard-mounted GPS. Even though both seniors knew the Twin Cities well, they were less sure about the suburbs. Equally important to the turn-by-turn directions was that the GPS would give Barry a continuously updated estimate of their time of arrival.

As they crossed into the suburb of Shakopee, Barry relaxed his shoulders. They were going to reach the high school in time.

Just barely.

A text arrived as they pulled into the front parking lot: *Stand by.*

Aaron made them sit for nearly an hour before sending the

next text. Beth read it aloud. "Drive to the tennis courts on the west side of the school. Look for a dented trash can. Remove the bag inside it. Fill it with all the money. Drop it back into the can."

"We're not gonna do that," Barry said. "Text back that he doesn't get the money until he releases Harry."

Beth sent the text and read the response when it arrived. "Harry is in a safe place. Give me half now."

Barry stroked his chin. "Aaron sounds desperate. Text that we'll give him a good-faith deposit of one thousand dollars. He'll get the rest when he turns over Harry."

Two minutes later, Beth read, "Five thousand dollars or you'll never see your son alive again."

Hot fear washed over Barry. He told himself that some fear was good, as long as he used it to fight back with cool confidence. Making eye-contact with Beth, he said, "I'm tempted to give Aaron the money, but we can't let him control the situation more than he already is. Text back that he either accepts three thousand dollars or we drive away."

Beth raised an eyebrow at Barry's bravado, sent the text, waited, and read the reply when it arrived. "Deal. Drop the money. Drive to the Target parking lot. Await further instructions."

Barry drove to the tennis courts and stopped next to the dented trash can. He scanned the area for an observer and noted that everyone must be in class, since not a single person was in sight.

Beth stepped onto the pavement carrying the ransom down payment, pulled the bag out of the trash can, dropped in the money, and lowered the bag back into the can.

Barry put the Mustang into gear as soon as Beth returned

to her seat. He remembered seeing the Target store on the way in and shook his head when Beth reached for his GPS. Driving directly to the store wasn't what he had in mind anyway. Instead, he detoured a short distance to the street in front of the Ford dealership and pulled over. Tilting his head toward Beth's smartphone, he said, "Jenny, I don't know if Aaron is retrieving the money himself or if he has an associate doing it. Either way, I'm gonna let you out of the trunk. I'm certain the backseat photo I sent to Aaron from the Gay 90s and any other observations he's made have convinced him that you aren't with us. Stay low and bring your blanket to hide under later, if necessary. We need to do this fast. Let me know once you've gathered everything you need, and I'll pop the trunk."

"I'm ready!" Jenny announced a moment later.

Beth opened her door and slid her seat forward.

Jenny climbed out, shut the trunk lid, and slithered into the backseat. "Whew!" she whistled. "It feels so good to get outta there."

"Having you in the trunk made me tense too," said Barry. "With all our racing around and sudden stops, I worried a rear-end accident could trap you inside."

"I hadn't thought of that. Now I'm doubly glad to be out of the trunk."

"Is everyone ready?" Barry asked.

"I am," said Jenny.

"Go ahead, dear," Beth said.

With a brief squeal of tires, Barry rushed them to the Target parking lot, where he grabbed a space near the perimeter. He switched off the car, and they waited.

And waited.

"I have to use the bathroom," Beth said.

"Me too," said Jenny.

Barry started the car and pointed. "I doubt anyone is watching us, but just in case, I'm gonna squeeze us into that open spot between the monster pickup and the van. Be careful not to ding my door when you get out."

Once the women eased onto the pavement, Barry stared at his smartphone, hoping a text with a ridiculous command didn't arrive while they were gone. Then it occurred to him that he could use a bathroom break too. He stuffed his phone into his back pocket and speed-walked to the store.

The next text didn't arrive until everyone had returned to the car and slipped into boredom: *Proceed to the White Bear Shopping Center in White Bear Lake. You have 35 minutes.*

Beth looked up the address on her phone and entered it into Barry's GPS. The device predicted a forty-five-mile drive that would take forty-seven minutes.

Barry glanced at the screen and protested, "That's ridiculous! If it were late at night, we might have a chance, but rush hour has already begun."

Jenny leaned forward. "I say, call Aaron's bluff. We still control the money he wants."

"I agree with Jenny," Beth said. "He's probably just fucking with us until it gets dark."

Barry accelerated out of the parking lot. "You're both probably correct, but Harry is my son. I'm not gonna ignore the text simply because it requires some fancy driving. Hold on!"

Human sounds accompanying the next thirty-five minutes included a variety of colorful interjections and shouts, accentuated by drawn-out screams of *"shiiit!"* Ultimately, driving from the southwestern suburb of Shakopee to the northeastern suburb of White Bear Lake during rush hour was impossible in the time allotted—at least for a seventy-one-year-old-man in his black Mustang.

They were roughly five minutes from their destination when the next text arrived. Beth read it aloud, "Stay where you are and wait for instructions."

Barry smirked. "Here on the freeway? In the middle of a traffic jam?"

Jenny leaned forward again. "One thing I've noticed while using my phone to observe the traffic camera feeds is that it takes a lot of concentration to pick out our car. My guess is that Aaron is already satisfied that no cops are shadowing us and isn't even bothering to watch the cameras anymore. Like Beth said, 'He's just fucking with us.'"

Nodding in agreement, Barry said under his breath, "I look forward to when it's our turn to do the fucking," and abandoned his plan to use the shoulder to pass the pack of vehicles in his way. Instead, he let the Mustang flow with the traffic until they reached the turnoff for the White Bear Shopping Center.

Upon their arrival, Beth looked around. "There's not much here. I was hoping we could grab some takeout."

Barry pointed as he drove through the parking lot. "There's a Taco Sven's."

"I'd rather go hungry," Beth declared.

Jenny tapped her phone. "There's supposed to be a Thai restaurant here somewhere."

Beth pointed. "There it is."

As Barry parked in front of the restaurant, Jenny brought up the menu and handed her phone to Beth. "Let me know what you guys want, and I'll go in and get it. If Aaron sends a text while I'm inside, we can decide whether to wait for our food or abandon our order."

When the sky darkened, the decision to have a meal proved to be a wise one. Since Aaron was going to make them wait, at least they could do it on full stomachs.

Troubling, however, was that the front edge of the snow-storm had arrived, and the temperature was dropping. Barry did his best to keep his windshield clear, and whenever one of the women complained about being too cold, he started the engine and cranked the heater.

Eventually Beth said, "We should take a chance and drive back to the Blue Loon Village. My all-wheel-drive Forester is better suited for this weather, and we could pick up some warmer clothes at the same time."

Barry was just about to agree when the next text arrived.

CHAPTER 30

Retribution Time

Beth read the text aloud. "Proceed to Valley Fair. It's the moment you've been waiting for. No time limit. Only Harry getting colder and colder. Ha! Ha!"

"Isn't that back in Shakopee?" Jenny asked.

Barry nodded. "Uh-huh. I don't think the high school and Valley Fair are more than five miles apart."

Jenny continued. "So, I'm guessing that Aaron has been in Shakopee the entire time. It takes a special kind of asshole to send us speeding all the way to White Bear Lake only to have us turn around and come right back."

"Oh, he's special all right," Beth deadpanned.

Barry steered out of the parking lot. "I was assuming we'd eventually end up in the woods somewhere, but from Aaron's point of view, what could be better than a big amusement park closed for the winter? He could have Harry tied up anywhere within the park, and if we don't do what he wants, it could take us hours to find him."

"Or," Beth surmised, "he could make us waste our time searching for Harry at Valley Fair, when he actually has him tied up at a nearby elementary school. He all but said he was gonna do the same thing to Harry that we did to him."

Barry tightened his grip on the steering wheel. "I hadn't thought of that! Replication would sweeten his revenge."

"How many elementary schools are there in Shakopee?" Beth asked.

Jenny tapped her smartphone screen. "I'm looking that up right now. . . . Five."

Barry fishtailed the Mustang onto the snow-covered highway. "Keep those addresses handy. I'll drive us to Valley Fair first. Once we get there, we'll decide what to do."

The Mustang didn't have snow tires. Now that Barry lived at the Blue Loon Village, he had no place to store an extra set of tires. Instead, he planned to do this winter what he'd done the previous winter, which was to rely on Beth's Subaru Forester with its all-weather tires whenever the streets became too slippery.

While driving as fast as he dared toward Shakopee, Barry considered Beth's suggestion of swinging by the Blue Loon Village to exchange the Mustang for the Forester. His next thought ruled out that idea. *The Forester doesn't have a trunk. If Aaron approaches when we arrive at Valley Fair, he could spot Jenny.*

Glancing into the rearview mirror, he said, "Jenny, once we hit Shakopee, I'm gonna pull over, so you can get back into the trunk. Beth, do you have the extra Mustang key in your purse?"

"Yes. It's on my key ring."

"Give it to Jenny. Also, put in your earbuds, make sure your hair covers them, and keep an open connection between your and Jenny's cell phones. That way she can hear what's happening and react appropriately."

"We seem more organized than usual," Beth said playfully.

Barry increased his speed. "With experience comes age."

Jenny laughed. "The correct phrase is 'with age comes experience.'"

"Whatever the case, no one fucks with the Silver Squad. Well, they do, but—shiiit!"

The Mustang spun to the left!

Barry steered left!

The women screamed!

The Mustang spun to the right!

Barry steered right and pumped the brakes!

Everyone screamed as they careened toward a pickup stalled on the shoulder.

Tink!

The Mustang—its tires catching the pavement just in time—collided into the pickup with the force of a teaspoon tapping a glass at a wedding reception.

As the women gulped for air, Barry shifted into reverse, slammed into drive, cleared the pickup, and screamed another "Shiiit!"

A semitruck filled his rearview mirror!

The Mustang's tires spun!

The semi's horn blasted!

In a moment that seemed to go in slow-motion, Barry lightened his touch on the accelerator until the rear tires took hold, allowing him to swerve the Mustang back onto the shoulder.

The semi roared by!

"Nice driving!" Jenny exclaimed.

"Is that sarcasm or a compliment?" Barry asked.

"A little of both," she replied.

Beth patted Barry's knee. "We can't save Harry if we all die before getting there."

Bringing the Mustang back up to the fastest speed that felt controllable, Barry replied, "I know, honey. I know."

* * *

Barry pulled over at the first Shakopee exit. Jenny gathered all her stuff, hopped onto the pavement, and climbed back into the trunk.

When they arrived at Valley Fair a few minutes later, the amusement park looked dark and eerie. Barry parked near the main entrance, looked at Beth, and said, "Button up. It's gonna be cold."

"Should I grab the gun from our vigilante tool kit?"

"What vigilante tool kit?"

"The one in the trunk."

"You mean the one I pulled out last night to make room for Jenny?"

"We're doing this unarmed?"

Jenny spoke into Beth's earbuds, "You can have my Glock."

Beth pointed to her ear. "Jenny offered us her gun."

"For now, I suggest we play by Aaron's rules and come without a weapon. Once we get Harry back, we'll switch to our rules."

Barry opened his door and stepped onto the parking lot. Beth did the same.

Noticing the sealed-off front entrance, Barry led Beth a little to their right. As they approached a perimeter fence that featured vertical black iron bars, he said, "Climbing this would be difficult, even for someone much younger than us, like Aaron." He glanced at his smartphone screen. "Still no text either."

"Maybe you should send Aaron a text to let him know we've arrived."

"There's no need," a voice called from the shadows on the opposite side of the fence. "Do you have my money?"

"It's in the car," Barry replied. "Do you have my son?"

"Get the money and we'll talk."

"I'll be back." Barry retrieved the duffel bag and approached the fence.

"Toss it over," Aaron demanded.

"Not until I see my son."

"He's not here."

"What do you mean, 'He's not here'?"

"He's somewhere else, getting colder by the second. As for me . . ." He ran his hands down the front of his green Army surplus parka. "I've got this nice warm coat, and I haven't seen a single person other than you two since I got here. Take all the time you want to think it over."

"Maybe I'll just call the cops," Barry growled.

"You're welcome to do that. But if the cops ever catch me, they'll put me away for a long time. Since my life would essentially be over, I will resist them with everything I've got. If they don't kill me during my arrest, I can promise that the trauma will give me temporary amnesia. Your fag son will be frozen solid by the time I remember where I hid him."

Barry charged the fence. "You motherfucker!"

Aaron stepped back and shook a finger. "Now, now. You wouldn't wanna give yourself a heart attack."

Beth put a hand on Barry's shoulder. "Just give him the money."

Barry scowled and threw the duffel bag over the fence.

Aaron caught it and used his smartphone flashlight to illuminate the inside. After confirming that the bag contained genuine bills and no exploding dye packs, he said, "I'll trust it's all here."

"It is. Now where's my son?"

"Remember a little over a year ago, when you two stripped me and left me tied to the monkey bars at a school?"

"You mean with the knife I left at your feet to cut yourself loose and the shoes and underwear I left for you at the curb?" Beth asked.

"Oh, you were *sooo* generous!" Aaron spat sarcastically. "There was more to it than that, and you know it."

"Yeah, like you beating your wife and children," Barry blurted.

Aaron narrowed his eyes. "Both of you. Take off all your clothes and back up to the fence. Now!"

"Why the hell would we do that?" Barry spat. "I gave you the money. Now you give me my son. That was our deal!"

"Was it? I only remember saying that we'd talk."

"We'll freeze to death," said Beth. "Do you want multiple murders on your hands?"

"I'll give you a chance, just like you gave me. I don't have a knife with me, so instead, I'll leave your cell phones just out of reach."

Barry sneered, "What good will that do if we can't reach them to call for help?"

Aaron stroked his chin. "Good point. Which one of you is more limber?"

"He is/She is," they said simultaneously.

"Do you both have cell phones?"

"Yes. But the battery died in mine, so I left it in the car," Beth said quickly.

"Then Barry's phone it is." He pointed. "When you back up to the fence, I'll only zip-tie your wrists. Then I'll climb over to the other side, stretch your pants out in front of you, and set your phone on the farthest leg. If you work carefully, you'll be able to pull the phone toward you and dial for help with your toes."

"Dial with my toes? What if I fail?"

Aaron pursed his lips. "I'll tell you what. To prove I'm more generous than either of you were to me, I'll leave Beth's feet unbound too. That way she can help you if necessary."

"This is a ridiculous discussion. I have a better idea." Barry looked at Beth and pointed to the Mustang with his thumb. Side by side, they walked backward until they halved their distance to the car. When they stopped, Barry held up his phone. "Since it's obvious you're not gonna honor your part of the deal, I'm gonna loop back to my original idea and call the cops. And if you climb over the fence before they arrive, I'll run you down with my Mustang and leave you pinned underneath until you tell me where my son is!"

Aaron's face contorted. "Fine! Here's a deal I will keep. I'll text you the location of your son, but only after I've guaranteed myself enough time to disappear. Which loops us back to both of you stripping and backing up to the fence."

"How can I be sure you'll actually send the text?"

Aaron grabbed a fence bar with each hand and growled through the gap, "I don't give a shit if your homo son takes it up the ass from every freak at that fag nightclub. God will deal with him. All I care about is just retribution for what you two did to me. Now if you want that text, strip and back up to the fence."

Beth glanced at Barry and nodded. They stepped forward.

As they removed their jackets and stripped, both did their best to gain any advantage they could. Anticipating that Aaron might check her pockets, Beth palmed her cellphone and used her body to block his view as she hid it in her bra. Barry preemptively placed his jeans onto the pavement, with its legs stretched out and his cell phone on the farthest leg. Their ultimate maneuver, however, was leaving their clothing far enough away from the fence to satisfy Aaron, but closer than he would have done had he placed the items himself.

Aaron looked his naked victims up and down. "One more thing. If the cops ultimately find me, I'd much rather go out in a shiny Mustang than the dull old beater I drove here. Give me the keys."

Barry leaned over—deliberately mooning Aaron—pulled the keys from his jacket pocket, scratched his balls with the same hand, and tossed the keys through the fence.

Then, as difficult as it was for them, Barry and Beth backed up to the fence and submitted their wrists for zip-tying around a vertical bar.

Once Aaron had them secured, he whistled. "That's quite a sight! My car is against the fence, way down the line. Now, Barry, I'm gonna climb up you to get out just like I climbed onto the roof of my car to get in. Lock your fingers together. They're my first step."

After tossing the duffel bag over the fence, Aaron stepped into Barry's hands, onto his head, swung over the top bar, and climbed down the opposite side. Then he retrieved the duffel bag, backed up, whistled again, and said, "See ya later, *Shiver Squad!*"

Beth watched Aaron strut to the Mustang. The moment he dropped into the driver's seat and shut the door, she called out, "Jenny! Stay in the trunk."

"Are you sure?" she whispered.

"Yes. We need to get the text with Harry's location before doing anything."

"What if Aaron doesn't send it?"

"Then you can press your Glock to his temple the next time he stops."

CHAPTER 31

Numb Nuts

As the Mustang departed the Valley Fair parking lot, Jenny asked, "Should I at least call the police?"

"Not yet," Beth replied. "My phone is on the ground, and I won't be able to answer your callback if you disconnect me. Right now, it's more important to keep an open connection."

"What if you get hypothermia?"

"Maintaining our connection will allow me to let you know if I feel that happening as we try to escape. In the meantime, I was born in northern Minnesota. This is nothin'."

"How's Barry doing?"

"He's so pissed; he's generating all the heat he needs."

"Okay. Going silent for now."

At the same time Beth was talking with Jenny, Barry was reaching out with his foot to pull the smartphone on his jeans closer. Once he could touch the phone with his toes, he realized how difficult it would be to even turn on the screen. Despite Beth's words, it didn't matter how pissed off he was or that he too was born in northern Minnesota, his feet and fingers were getting numb. Also, much to his embarrassment, a certain extremity was shrinking smaller than he'd ever seen it.

Deciding to change tactics, he attempted to rub through his zip tie by lowering himself into a crouch and then raising himself to his tiptoes. "The bar between my wrists feels smooth," he said with a grimace. "How 'bout yours?"

Beth mimicked Barry's maneuver. "Mine feels smooth too."

"We knew getting zip-tied was a possibility. Why didn't we prepare for it?"

"I did. The nail clipper I used to escape Aaron's loft is stashed in the front pocket of my pants. Unfortunately, I didn't anticipate having to hide my cell phone in my bra. I could only do so much maneuvering with Aaron watching us so closely."

Barry used his nose to point at Beth's pants. "You have a nail clipper in there?"

"That's what I said. Why don't you be a gentleman and retrieve it for us?"

Barry sighed and lowered himself all the way to the ground. Doing his best to ignore the prickly pebbles and slushy snow assaulting his skin, he hooked a toe onto Beth's pants and pulled them to him. "Right or left pocket?"

"Right."

He reached inside with his toes. "There's nothing in there!"

"Try the other right pocket."

"Do you mean the left one?"

She offered an innocent shrug.

Barry contorted his foot one way and then the other until he grasped the nail clipper. Once confident he had a firm grip between his toes, he extracted the clipper. Standing again was a challenge, but after an initial failed attempt, he developed a technique of grabbing the bars behind his back, pushing up, holding, raising his grip, and repeating. When he was finally upright, he attempted to bring his foot to his hands by flexing his leg backward between the bars. "Ow! Ow! Ow!" he cried, lowering his foot.

"What's wrong?"

"Leg cramp!"

"Do you want me to take over?"

"Give me a second. I wanna try again." He took a few deep breaths and bent his leg backward. "Ow! Ow! Ow!"

"We don't have time to wait for your cramp to go away."

"It's not a cramp this time. The bars are squeezing my thigh. It might be stuck."

"Seriously?"

Barry wiggled. "If I pull back with all my strength, I think I can free my thigh. However, I'm afraid I'll send the nail clipper flying at the same time."

"Pass the clipper to me."

"Are you sure?"

"Yes. I can get my entire leg through the bars."

"Okay, but don't drop it."

"No shit," Beth said sarcastically. She glanced over her shoulder. "I want you to twist your body as far away from me as you can. That'll bring your foot closer to mine."

Barry did as she said.

"There. Now stay perfectly still and don't release the nail clipper until I say so." She brought her foot next to his, then lowered it to grasp the clipper from below. "I've almost got it. Just a little . . . Now!"

He released his grip.

She dropped it.

Ping!

The coating of snow muffled the ping produced by the clipper when it hit the ground, but it was a ping nevertheless.

"Damn it!" Beth cried.

Barry freed his leg. "Did you see where it landed?"

"No."

"I told you—"

"Shut up!" She pulled her leg back through the bars and scanned the ground.

The coating of snow dimmed the glint produced by a security light when it reflected off the clipper, but it was a glint nevertheless.

"Found it!" Beth proclaimed.

She stretched her leg back through the bars and cautiously pulled the nail clipper closer. Once she had the clipper where she wanted it, she grasped it between her toes, stood, and brought it to her hands.

She smiled at Barry, said, "I've got it," and raised her voice. "Jenny, did you hear that?"

"Yes."

"My fingers are numb, so it may take me a while to work through our zip ties." She leaned against the bars and slid to the ground, lessening the chance of losing the nail clipper if she dropped it while cutting.

Barry commented, "Once we escape, maybe—"

"Shhh!" Beth interrupted. "I need to concentrate."

As Beth worked, Barry stared straight ahead, feeling too self-conscious to look down. He concentrated on positive thoughts: *At least Michelangelo isn't around to paint my full-length portrait.*

"I'm free!" Beth announced a moment later. She stepped forward, slipped into her jacket, and retrieved her phone.

"Hey! What about me?" Barry asked.

Beth smiled and aimed her phone.

"Don't you dare!"

Dropping the phone into her jacket pocket, she rubbed her hands together and said, "Turn as far to the side as you can."

Beth cut Barry loose, and after they got dressed, she called out, "Jenny, we're both free. How are you doing?"

"Just bumping along in the dark. Should one of us call the police?"

Beth looked at Barry. "Should we call the police?"

He pushed the side button on his phone and tapped the screen. "There's no text from Aaron yet. I know that his having the conscience to send one is a long shot, but it's still our best chance to find Harry. In the meantime, let's find Aaron's car. Shakopee isn't that big. If we get lucky, and he left a key, we can quickly check out all the elementary schools."

"Wouldn't the police be able to search for Harry faster?" Beth asked.

"Sure, but they'd also quickly hunt down Aaron in my Mustang. What if he makes a run for it and gets killed or seriously injured in a high-speed chase? We need to make sure he's capable of being interrogated until the moment we find my son."

"Did you hear that, Jenny?" Beth asked.

"Uh-huh. It's risky, but I don't wanna die in a high-speed chase either."

Barry cupped his hands around his mouth and yelled, "Harryyy!" He listened for an answer and tried again. "Harryyy!"

"Are you thinking he could be tied up somewhere within

the park?" Beth asked.

"It would be difficult for Aaron to maintain control of Harry while forcing him over the fence, so I doubt it. Still, yelling doesn't hurt anything."

Beth took a deep breath and screamed, "Harryyy!" Softening her voice, she added, "Oops! Sorry about that, Jenny."

Barry rubbed Beth's shoulder with one hand while pointing at the fence with the other. "You walk that way, and I'll walk this way. Whoever reaches the car drives back to pick up the other."

"That is, if it's possible to start it."

"I'll say a little prayer to the SPAM Gods," Barry said with a nervous smile.

Roughly one hundred yards into her walk, Beth spotted the old Kia K5 alongside the fence. She broke into a run and, upon reaching the car, opened the door and checked the ignition. No keys. She also checked above the visor, under the floor mat, and in the glove compartment. Nothing.

"Jenny! I've found the car. No luck with the keys, however. I'm gonna hang up and call Barry. I'll ring you back."

"Okay."

Beth tapped the icon to dial Barry.

He answered with an immediate, "Did you find the car?"

"Yes. But I couldn't find—"

Thump!

Thump! Thump! Thump!

"Someone's in the trunk!" she exclaimed.

Thump! Thump! Thump!

"Is it Harry?" he asked.

"It must be. Since I've only met your son once, and he could be naked, you should be the first person he sees."

"You've met him twice," he corrected.

"No matter how many times I've met him, you should be here."

"I'm on my way!"

CHAPTER 32

Racing Past Stars

Barry arrived with surprising speed. Out of breath, he huffed, "Har . . . Harry? It's . . . Dad. Are you in there?"

Thump! Thump! Thump!

"Pop the trunk!" he yelled.

Beth leaned into the car and pulled the release.

The scene, illuminated by the trunk light, was intended to be as much of a shock for whoever opened the trunk as it was to be cruel to Harry. At worst, Barry had expected to find his son naked. Instead, he was wearing his drag queen stage clothes, with his arms and legs hogtied with zip ties, and duct tape covering his mouth. Written across the tape in red ink were the words "I suck cock." Completing the scene was a giant rubber penis, strategically duct taped to his chest.

Barry lifted Harry into a sitting position and ripped the tape from his mouth and chest. "Beth! I need your nail clipper!"

"I'm tied up in a trunk, and you're worried about my nails?" Harry said with a smirk. "Believe me, my nails are perfect!"

Beth looked away as she handed the clipper to Barry. "Is he naked?"

"No."

She glanced into the trunk. "Nice to see you again, Harry."

"You too, Ms. Potter. We should get together more often." He peered through the fence and recognized where he was. "Maybe when the water rides aren't frozen."

While Barry worked on Harry's restraints, Beth stepped aside and reconnected with Jenny. "We found Harry!"

"How is he?"

"As sarcastic as his father is."

"That's good. . . . I think."

"Where are you?"

"According to the GPS on my phone, we're heading north on I-35."

"Aaron could be making a run for Canada. Now that we have Harry, you should call the highway patrol and let them know where you are."

"Hmm. . . . That feels like the most logical thing to do. However, I'm curious about where Aaron is headed and nervous about what he might do if the cops try to pull him over. In this snowy weather, dealing with the boredom of riding in the trunk at a safe speed is preferable to the excitement of clinging to the side of the trunk during a car chase. If Aaron is indeed heading for Canada, he'll have to stop for gas before reaching the border. That might be a good time to pop out and introduce him to my Glock."

"It's your call, dear. Barry and I will follow as soon as we are able."

"That sounds good. In the meantime, I recommend we disconnect our open connection to save battery power."

"I agree. Call me if anything changes." Beth slid her phone into her pocket and turned to see Barry and Harry locked in a warm embrace. "Aw. . . . The father and son are reunited!"

Barry draped his coat over Harry's shoulders, stepped back, and looked him in the eyes. "Can I still refer to you as my son?"

"Of course. I'm not transgender. I'm just a normal gay man who makes outstanding tips by performing in drag."

"Sorry. Sometimes I get confused by all the sexual variations people have these days."

"We've always been here, Dad. You're just old."

"Old? Before we escaped and rescued you, your future stepmother and I were stripped naked and zip-tied to a fence. Biologically, we're both seventy-one, but I'll have you know that neither of us identifies as a day older than sixty-nine."

"You two are getting married?"

"She hasn't said yes yet, but one of these days she will."

Harry laughed.

Beth brushed the newly fallen snow from her shoulders. "Let's not stand here, freezing our asses off. I just finished talking with Jenny. She's still riding in the Mustang's trunk, possibly heading for Canada, and prefers that we hold off on calling the cops. So instead, I'm calling a taxi. Once we get to the Blue Loon Village, we can check in with Jenny and follow her in the Forester."

Harry threw back his shoulders. "I was kidnapped, and you two were zip-tied to a fence! No matter what Jenny says, we must call the cops."

Beth shot Barry a defiant look before shifting her gaze to Harry.

Barry snorted. "Trust me, son. When you see your future stepmother—or any other woman for that matter—glaring at you like that, just lower your head and comply."

Harry relaxed his shoulders. "Fine. But out here, an Uber will be cheaper and faster than a taxi."

* * *

Beth checked in with Jenny the moment she stepped out of the Uber and relayed to the men what she learned as they rode up the elevator. "The Mustang is still on I-35, a little beyond the northern suburbs. Jenny thinks the road conditions must be getting worse, because they've slowed down substantially after what felt like a fishtail."

"Aaron has probably never driven a rear-wheel-drive car before," Barry said with a slight chuckle.

Everyone stepped out of the elevator and hurried down the hall.

As they entered Barry's apartment, Beth said, "If we're quick here, we have a chance to catch them with my Forester."

"Only if you let me drive," Barry said.

"Isn't that a bit sexist?" Harry asked.

"No. Not at all. You've only witnessed my *dad-speed driving*. She, on the other hand, has witnessed my *dad-on-speed driving*. And I happen to be pretty good at it."

"He's right," Beth said. "And I enjoy being the navigator."

Barry pulled his warmest winter coat from the closet and handed it to Harry. Then he reached for his wallet and said, "Here's some money for an Uber. Or if you prefer, you're welcome to stay here. Your future stepmother and I will be back after we finish this thing."

Harry grimaced as he slipped into the coat. "Aside from the fact that you have no sense of style, there's absolutely no way you're going without me."

Barry looked down. "In stiletto pumps?"

"My feet are bigger than yours. I doubt you have anything that'll fit me."

"Oh yeah, I do." He leaned back into his closet and pulled out some classic Minnesota footwear.

"Snowmobile boots!" Harry laughed as he kicked off his heels. "They're gonna clash with my dress."

* * *

Freshly armed with their vigilante tool kit, warm clothing, and road snacks, the Silver Squad and the Son of Silver Squad raced north in Beth's Subaru Forester. Under normal driving conditions, catching a car with such a significant head start would have been almost impossible. But on this night, nothing was normal.

* * *

From early in his journey, Aaron regretted not sticking with his front-wheel drive Kia. Despite his bravado at Valley Fair, the Mustang terrified him. He had barely depressed the Mustang's accelerator when the burst of rear-wheel-drive power nearly spun him off the slippery freeway. He was also more nervous about getting caught than he had let on. Had he stuck with his Kia, he would have had a better chance of blending in with the traffic and avoiding arrest. When his frustration peaked over his lack of foresight, he slammed his forehead against the steering wheel and almost lost control again. He took a deep breath and slowed way down.

* * *

Once Beth resumed contact with Jenny, she was able to estimate where they'd catch up with the Mustang. At current speeds, that spot was near Silver Bay, roughly two hundred miles to the north. That is, if Aaron was truly heading for Canada and not some other destination.

Beth had previously set up the sound system in her Forester to take over her smartphone automatically. That allowed hands-free communication with Jenny that everyone in the car could hear easily.

Harry inquired, "Wouldn't Aaron need a passport to get into Canada?"

"Not necessarily," said Barry. "A passport card could get him into Canada too. That's something he may have carried with him since long before he became homeless. And although I don't know if they exist anymore, there used to be some un-guarded back roads across the border."

"Does Aaron's ultimate destination even matter to us?" Jenny asked. "My original plan was to jump out the first time he stopped. Now that you guys are following, wouldn't it be safer to stay in the trunk until you catch up—no matter where that is?"

Barry adjusted his rearview mirror so he could see his son as he spoke. "Did Aaron have a gun?"

"Yes," Harry replied. "He never would've been able to re-strain me or force me into the trunk without pointing one at me."

Barry raised his voice. "Jenny, he has a—"

"I heard," she interrupted.

"Then I agree that you should wait until we catch up. Beth grabbed the vigilante tool kit when we stopped at the Blue Loon Village. Two guns against one might convince Aaron to surrender willingly."

"Okay, we'll go with that plan—at least until Silver Bay or the equivalent distance. If you don't catch up by then, my bladder is gonna force an alternative plan."

"I'm driving as fast as I dare."

"In the meantime, let's go back to saving battery power. I'm gonna disconnect and try to take a nap. Call me if you catch the Mustang before I wake up, and I'll call you if anything changes here in the trunk."

"Sweet dreams," Beth said.

"Could Jenny be tired because of lack of oxygen in the trunk?" Harry asked.

"No," said Barry. "When you were in the trunk, claustrophobia and having to breathe through your nose may have made it feel that way. Automobile trunks don't seal that tight."

"Says the only one of us who hasn't spent time in a trunk this week," Beth deadpanned.

* * *

As the storm's intensity increased, falling snow reflected in the Forester's headlights, making Barry feel as if he were piloting a spaceship that was racing past stars in a science-fiction movie. Aside from the reduced visibility, the snow had a mesmerizing effect on Harry and Beth. No one said a word until Jenny's call jolted them back to reality.

Beth answered. "Is everything okay?"

"I'm in Duluth," she whispered.

"Why are you whispering?" Barry asked.

"Because there's no engine noise to mask my voice. I think we've stopped for gas."

"If that's the case, we're about twenty-five minutes behind you. If Aaron takes his time there, I can close the gap even more."

"Aren't you going to need gas, too?"

Barry glanced at the fuel gauge. "We're okay for now. If he continues to Canada, there are plenty of small towns with gas stations along the way."

Beth spoke up. "I've been thinking about alternative destinations for Aaron. He could head for the Iron Range, or, more likely, turn onto Highway 2 on the far side of Two Harbors. That would take him into a lake-filled area with a ton of cabins that are closed up for the winter. If he broke into one of those, he could disappear for months."

Harry leaned forward. "Wouldn't he need to stop for supplies if he's gonna do that?"

Beth looked back. "There's a lot we don't know. But if I were Aaron, and my plan was to break into a cabin, I'd take advantage of the cover provided by this snowstorm, grab some basics at a gas station convenience store, and worry about supplies later."

"Let's hope that's the case," Jenny whispered. "Because if Aaron picks up anything that necessitates opening the trunk, he and I will have our confrontation no matter where you guys are."

Barry risked adding a couple more miles-per-hour to his speed.

After a few minutes of silence, Jenny said, "We're moving. I'm disconnecting again to save battery power. I'll call back the moment I have something new to report."

I-35 ends in Duluth, where it becomes MN 61 and continues one hundred fifty miles northeast to the Canadian border. The Forester was two miles beyond Duluth when Jenny called again. "I think we can cross Canada off the list. When I felt the Mustang turn, I checked the GPS on my phone. We're now on Highway 2, just as Beth had predicted."

Beth tapped a map app on her phone. "The good news is that Aaron's new presumed destination is much closer than Canada."

"Assuming you're correct," Barry added, "I'm now curious whether he has a key to a cabin or intends to break into one."

"I felt better about this when Canada was his presumed destination," Jenny lamented. "Even if Aaron had driven there with no additional stops, my popping out of the trunk in front of customs agents at the border would've been a safe option. Now, I'm wondering if I should've confronted him in Duluth. This would all be over by now."

"I'm glad you didn't do that," Beth said. "Had you confronted Aaron at the gas station, it could have devolved into a gunfight. While I have no doubt you would've prevailed, what if a bystander got hit in the process, or someone decided to live out his good guy with a gun fantasy and judged you as the bad guy?"

Jenny sighed. "I suppose you're right. I just hope he chooses a cabin that's not hours away. Pretty soon I'm gonna have to pee like a son of a bitch."

Barry checked the fuel gauge again and said, "If I remember correctly, gas stations are rare on Highway 2. I'm gonna make a quick stop in Two Harbors to fill up the tank."

* * *

While Barry filled the Forester at the Circle K gas station, Harry and Beth hurried to the bathroom. Since Harry usually restricted his drag appearances to parties and the Gay 90s, he hesitated for a moment in front of the men's room door. Had he been in Minneapolis, he wouldn't have given his appearance a second thought, but in small-town Two Harbors he stuffed his wig into a coat pocket, opened the door, lifted the front of his dress, and stepped up to a urinal.

The Circle K gas station sat at the intersection of MN 61 and the street that would eventually become Highway 2. From there, they would head directly north.

They were three miles outside of Two Harbors when Jenny called. "We've turned again and are now heading west on the Wales Road."

Barry replied, "Ah, the road to Brimson. I know where that is. We're less than fifteen minutes behind you. Wait a minute. . . ." He squinted. "Now that we're moving away from Lake Superior, the snow is letting up. I might be able to go a little faster."

As Jenny disconnected, Barry brought the Forester up to a satisfying hum.

Harry adjusted his seatbelt and said, "Dad, I'm seeing a side of you I've never seen before. It's one thing to hear stories about your exploits with the Silver Squad; it's quite another to see you in action. You've always been a hero to me, but now your heroism is more than just a father-son thing. It's actually legit!"

Barry swallowed hard and said, "Don't forget about your future stepmother."

"Oh, I knew she was legit the moment I met her!"

Silence filled the car as Barry concentrated on the highway, and Beth watched for their turn. Upon reaching Wales Road, Barry veered left and accelerated back up to speed.

Shortly thereafter, Jenny called with another update. "We've turned onto the Thomas Lake Road. Don't confuse it with the South Thomas Lake Road, which comes up first. As near as I can tell from my map app, the road goes most of the way around the lake before it dead-ends. Is there fresh snow on the ground?"

"Yes," Beth answered.

"Then, hopefully, you can follow our tracks to wherever we're going. How far are you behind me?"

Beth looked at the map on Barry's GPS. "Maybe ten minutes."

"Okay. I'll try not to get into a gun—" The phone disconnected.

CHAPTER 33

Footprints

Beth attempted to call Jenny back, but the call went directly to voicemail.

Ten minutes later, Barry spotted a single set of automobile tracks leading from Wales Road onto Thomas Lake Road. Even without Jenny's help, following the Mustang would be easy.

Aside from those tracks, if Aaron intended to break into a cabin, he had happened upon the ideal time of year to do so. Summer and fall activities were over, yet several more weeks of cold weather would be necessary before Thomas Lake froze deep enough for ice fishing.

Barry followed the tracks two-thirds of the way around the lake before they veered into a driveway bordered by thick forest. He drove in a short distance, changed his mind, retreated to the road, turned around, and backed down the driveway toward what he assumed would be a lakeside cabin.

Due in part to his arthritic neck, Barry's backward driving skills weren't as proficient as his forward driving skills were.

After multiple near collisions with bordering pine trees, Beth blurted, "Give it up and stop here! We'll walk the rest of the way."

Before departing the Forester, Beth opened the vigilante tool kit and grabbed two flashlights. She also pocketed the tiny pistol they had acquired a year earlier during an otherwise unprofitable robbery. While handing one of the flashlights to Barry, she said, "I've got the pistol. Do you want the stun gun?"

"Why would I need that when you and Jenny each have a gun?" He thought for a moment. "Give it to Harry. That way he'll have something for defense. Later, if the situation calls for an unarmed negotiator, I'll take that job."

The father, son, and future stepmother eased out of the Forester with as much stealth as they could muster. From there, they slunk down the long driveway until reaching a clearing that revealed the Mustang parked behind a well-lit, two-level cabin made from peeled logs stained golden. A five-foot-high porch wrapped around the entire cabin, and outbuildings included a boathouse, a shed, and a sauna. In all, the cabin appeared to be too upscale for a man who had spent most of the previous year homeless.

Barry said softly, "We don't need our flashlights. I'm turning mine off. Beth, you should do the same."

Beth flicked off her flashlight, dropped it into a pocket, and pulled out her smartphone. She attempted to call Jenny again. When nothing happened, she looked at the top right corner of her screen and said, "We're too deep in the woods for cell phone service."

Barry grasped Beth's shoulder with his left hand and did the same to Harry with his right. "Both of you hang back in the shadows," he whispered. "I'm gonna sneak up to the Mustang and let Jenny know she can come out."

He hunched over and hurried to the Mustang. He was just about to tap on the trunk lid when he glanced at the ground. A floodlight mounted on the peak of the nearest outbuilding illuminated two sets of footprints in the snow. One set was smaller than the other.

The trunk lid popped open.

Barry didn't have to peer into the trunk to know it was empty.

"She's up here!" Aaron shouted from the back porch.

Barry cringed as he looked up. Aaron had Jenny restrained in a neck hold, the Glock he'd snatched from her pressed against her temple. A second gun, a rifle, was slung across his back, its barrel peeking over his shoulder.

"I'm so glad you escaped in time to join the party!" Aaron said, dropping the key fob onto the porch. "If the weather hadn't forced me to turn off the radio to concentrate, I never would've heard your blonde friend's voice inside the trunk. Where's Beth?"

"She's back in the Twin Cities, talking with the police."

"Bullshit." He raised his voice. "Beth, Beth, come out, come out, wherever you are! If I don't see you in five seconds, I'm blowing a hole in Blondie's head!"

Beth stepped out of the dark forest. "I'm right here. You have no conflict with Jenny. Let's do a trade. Her for me. I'll even promise not to escape if you have a sudden urge to make a run for the outhouse."

"Fat chance. Now where's the homo?"

Barry balled his fists. "What are you, thirteen? One thing's for sure. You're lucky to have escaped murder charges. When you didn't send the text with Harry's location, we caught a ride to the Blue Loon Village and raced after you in Beth's car. We also called the cops. Fortunately, they found Harry just in time. He's now in the hospital being treated for severe hypothermia."

"Lucky? The only ones with any luck are you two." He flashed a threatening smile. "But now that we're way out here, that's about to end."

Barry approached the porch, deciding to change tactics and trust the right words would come out of his mouth. "This is a beautiful cabin. You obviously didn't lose it when you got divorced. Why didn't you just move here instead of living on the streets?"

Aaron vibrated his lips. "I wish it was mine. It belongs to my ex-wife's parents. I drove here because I'd visited it enough times to know where they hide the key and keep their guns."

Now on the bottom step, Barry spread his arms to show Aaron he wasn't carrying a weapon. "Here's an idea. As things stand now, Beth and I got what we wanted, which was to protect your ex-wife and children from a stressful and painful life. You also got what you wanted, which was revenge against Beth and me by making us freeze our asses off at Valley Fair. On top of that, you got twenty thousand dollars out of the deal. Right now, I'd say you're the winner. But if you kill someone, there's no doubt you'll be caught and spend the rest of your life in prison. So how 'bout if you let Jenny go, take my Mustang on a back road into Canada, and start a new life? The title is in the glove compartment. I'll even sign it over to you."

"How stupid do you think I am?" he spat. "You'll call the cops the moment I leave."

"With what? There's no cell phone service here, and if the cabin has a landline, your ex-in-laws likely had it suspended for the winter. Go ahead and check."

"You said you followed me in Beth's car. What about that?"

"We'll puncture a tire."

He chuckled. "What'll that give me? A half-hour head start?"

"We'll puncture all four if it'll make you feel better. But at some point, you're gonna have to take a risk. That is, if you don't want to spend the rest of your life in prison."

"Nah. Now that you've laid it out for me, I think I'll just kill you all. I hadn't put any thought into Canada, but with the money you gave me and two cars to choose from, that's not a bad idea. My ex-in-laws won't come up here until the ice is thick enough for their fish house, so there's little risk in me hanging out at the cabin until things die down."

Beth raised her gun as she stepped forward. "What if I shoot you first?"

Aaron chuckled. "With that little thing? You're more likely to hit Blondie than me."

She took another step and steadied her aim with both hands. "Maybe. But if you're gonna kill her anyway, I might as well give it a try. So how about it, Aaron? Do you feel lucky?"

"Hold it!" Barry shouted, waving his arms. "I can't believe this stupidity!"

"Stupidity?" Aaron asked. "It's just getting exciting! Aren't you curious about whether Beth will actually shoot? And if she does, will she hit me, hit Blondie, or just shatter the glass in the door behind us?"

Barry nodded. "I admit some curiosity as to how that would play out. But the stupidity I'm referring to isn't about Beth risking a shot. It's that you've allowed us to distract you again. Just like we did last year." His eyes flitted to the side. "Push hard!"

Zzzap!

Aaron dropped the Glock!

Jenny dropped Aaron with an elbow and a kick!

Barry scooped up the Glock and dislodged the rifle before grinning down at Aaron and saying, "Cool wrap-around porch! You remember my son, Harry, don't you?"

Harry thumbed the safety on the stun gun and shook a playful finger. "Aaron, you dirty boy. Stop looking up my dress!"

As Jenny took her Glock back from Barry, she tilted her head and asked, "Did Beth just quote *Dirty Harry*?"

He chuckled. "Yeah. She does that when she's trying to sound tough. Or sometimes, when she's feeling amorous, she'll say, 'Go ahead, make my day!'"

"Dad!" Harry cringed. "That's way too much information."

"Totally!" said Jenny.

CHAPTER 34

The Handoff

The return trip to the Twin Cities would follow the same route with two additional stops. Once Barry and Harry secured Aaron with zip ties from the vigilante tool kit, they stuffed him into the backseat of the Mustang and discovered the ransom money behind the driver's seat at the same time.

"Men in the Mustang; women in the Forester?" Barry asked.

"I was going to suggest the same thing," Beth said. "We'll alert the Two Harbors Police Department and Detective Sorenson that we're dropping off Aaron as soon as we get close enough to catch a cell phone signal. They're gonna want statements from all of us."

"After that, let's check into a hotel. I'm too tired to drive all the way back to the Twin Cities."

"I agree. We're all running on adrenaline at the moment. None of us should be behind the wheel when that adrenaline crashes."

* * *

Over the years, Barry and Harry had drifted apart. Even though some of their relatives had speculated it was because Barry had difficulty accepting that his only son was gay, that wasn't the case. Sometimes there's no reason for such drifts, other than the ebb and flow of father and son relationships and differing lifestyles that seldom cross paths.

Despite the anguish everyone experienced during the past few days, Barry knew his memories of those days would also include some warm feelings. He got to be a hero in the eyes of his son, and his son got to be a hero in his eyes, too. Though if asked, each would say the other was a hero long before Aaron interrupted their lives.

What that meant was that both men were enjoying some quality father and son time as they traveled side-by-side in the shiny black Mustang. Sure, a violent wife-beater-kidnapper was in the backseat, but all Barry had to do was wave a roll of duct tape in the air to guarantee they wouldn't hear from him for the remainder of the trip.

Delivering Aaron to the Two Harbors Police Department was a big deal. Barry didn't know how many people worked there, but he guessed that word had gotten around, enticing many of the employees to push themselves out of bed to witness the late-night handoff. Since Detective Sorenson had already dispatched a deputy to pick up Aaron and return him to the Twin Cities, Aaron's stop at the Lake County Jail would be brief.

Unfortunately for Barry, Beth, Jenny, and Harry, brief wasn't part of the transfer for them. Each had to give separate sworn statements corroborating what happened, and even then, the Two Harbors police chief delayed their release until Detective Sorenson vouched for them.

Adding to the difficult night was finding a hotel where a front desk clerk was on duty to check them in. Apparently, check-ins at four in the morning weren't all that common in Two Harbors. Nevertheless, everyone got a few hours of sleep before traveling south.

* * *

Barry dropped off Harry at his downtown apartment before proceeding to the Blue Loon Village. When he entered his own apartment, Beth and Jenny were already sitting at the counter sipping their coffees. Grabbing a stool, he asked, "Did you make enough for me?"

"Of course," said Jenny, reaching for the carafe.

As Barry warmed his hands on the cup Jenny poured for him, he asked her, "Are you gonna stick around for a while?"

"I'm thinking about heading home tomorrow morning," she said.

Beth swiveled on her stool. "Why don't you stay for a few more days? As family."

Jenny looked at Barry. "Now that I've gotten to know Harry a little, I'd love to see his show. Do you know when he performs again?"

Barry pulled out his smartphone. After multiple taps and a single swipe, he said, "Tomorrow night."

"Then I'll stay an extra day. Let's eat dinner downtown and walk over to the Gay 90s afterward."

Barry rubbed his eyes. "You know I don't have a problem

with Harry's sexual orientation. I'm not sure, however, if I'm ready to see him dancing in a dress on stage. That part of his life is brand new to me."

Jenny slid a napkin under her cup and said, "Well, since none of us are gonna feel like doing much tonight, how about we make some popcorn and prepare you for Harry's performance by streaming some movies? I'm not an expert on drag queen movies, but I remember enjoying *The Birdcage* and *To Wong Foo, Thanks for Everything! Julie Newmar*."

"I haven't seen the second one," Beth said. "But I saw *The Birdcage* many years ago and thought it was wonderful."

"Then let's start with that one," Jenny suggested. "After that, if we feel awake enough for a double feature, we'll give *To Wong Foo, Thanks for Everything! Julie Newmar* a try."

"Is that okay with you, Barry?" Beth asked.

"Sure," he said, pushing aside his coffee. "But if I don't take a nap first, I'll be lucky to make it through the opening credits."

* * *

Barry had just fallen asleep when his cell phone rang. Without opening his eyes, he flung his arm toward the bedside table where his fingers walked to the offending device and squeezed random buttons until silence was restored.

At the same time, Beth and Jenny lounged on opposite ends of the couch with their stockinged feet meeting near the center of the coffee table. Jenny was busy on her laptop computer, catching up on work she had tossed aside when she rushed north after Beth's abduction. Beth was reading a novel, pausing every few paragraphs to rest her exhausted eyelids.

Both jerked when Beth's cell phone rang.

Grabbing her phone from the side table, she said, "Hello, this is Beth. . . . Uh-huh. . . . Uh-huh. . . . Yes. . . . A cabin. . . . Thomas Lake. . . . Near Brimson. . . . Yes. The same guy. . . . A stun gun. . . . It's a long story. . . . I know, but I'm exhausted. . . . Why don't you call me tomorrow? . . . How about ten? . . . Goodbye."

Before she could return her phone to the side table, it rang again. Raising an eyebrow at Jenny, she answered, "Hello, this is Beth. . . ."

The second call went much like the first one, only this time Beth ended the conversation by turning off her phone.

Jenny rubbed her forehead. "Apparently, we're gonna be in the news again."

Beth shrugged. "How could we not be? I'd just like to delay the inevitable until tomorrow. At least it'll give us an excuse to talk with the media about Kayleigh again."

An embarrassed expression washed over Jenny's face. "With everything that's happened, I'd stopped thinking about her."

"See how that works?"

Jenny nodded. "Yeah. I'm a politician's wet dream. Flood the zone, and I'll forget what happened the day before."

CHAPTER 35

License to Kill

Barry's nap was a success! So was his popcorn making. And just like humorous books can ease stress, humorous movies can do the same. For most, anyway.

For Barry, the movies they streamed only redirected his stress. While he now felt prepared for the shock of seeing Harry perform in drag, he doubted he was prepared for the parental issues that were more traditional. Should he cheer on his son wildly, like a groupie? Or should he act reserved, to avoid causing embarrassment? What if his emotions overcame him, like a proud parent at a graduation or wedding ceremony? Would Harry interpret his tears as shame?

Eventually, Barry decided the best way to deal with his new dilemma was to get a good night's sleep. He pushed up from the couch and said, "Goodnight, you two."

"I'll join you in a minute," said Beth.

Jenny offered Barry a little wave and commented, "Don't forget to charge your cell phone tonight. I have a hunch our phones are gonna be ringing like crazy tomorrow."

"Oh, gee, thanks," he said sarcastically before disappearing down the hall.

* * *

After eating breakfast downstairs in the dining room, Barry, Beth, and Jenny carried their coffees up to the apartment and sat on their usual stools at the counter. There they held up their cell phones, thumbs poised on the power buttons. Barry counted down, "Three, two, one!"

Moments later, their voicemail indicators started flashing, and three different ringtones began chiming.

Beth soon concluded that answering calls and voicemails was too inefficient for their situation. Pounding an open palm on the counter, she shouted, "Barry! Jenny! This is ridiculous. Tell everyone you speak to that we're having a news conference downstairs at eleven-thirty."

"Better yet," said Barry as he tapped his phone, "we should put that message on our voicemails and let the calls roll to that."

* * *

Samantha shook a finger at Beth after learning that the Blue Loon Village would be hosting a news conference on short notice. "You need to check with me first about these things. What if we were already using the lobby for some other activity?"

Beth shrugged. "Sorry. One of these days, Barry and I will regress to being sedentary old folks, and you'll miss how we've kept you entertained."

Samantha laughed. "Of that I have no doubt!"

Ultimately, the news conference proceeded much like the others, only with their new adventures to discuss. Barry, Beth, and Jenny recapped Harry's abduction, their back-and-forth races across the Twin Cities, paying the ransom, the ice-cold strip show at Valley Fair, Jenny's trunk ride, capturing Aaron at Thomas Lake, recovering the ransom money, and delivering Aaron to the Two Harbors Police Department.

Beth was transitioning to the subject of Kayleigh when a reporter with salt-and-pepper hair and a mustache waved to get her attention. She stopped and asked, "Yes?"

"You obviously haven't heard what happened."

Beth tensed. "Oh, shit."

The reporter continued. "I called Kayleigh's mother, Emma Clark, late yesterday afternoon to get a quote to include in a feature I'm writing about the state of health insurance in Minnesota. Emma was in a hospital waiting room when she answered. Kayleigh had a dizzy spell while entering her bathroom and hit her head when she fell."

"Is she gonna be okay?"

"I don't know. Kayleigh was being prepped for surgery when I called. Obviously, Emma had more important things to do than divulge medical details to a reporter. I plan to follow up with another call later today. If you'd like, I can contact you when I have more information."

"That won't be necessary. I'll call Emma myself. Thank you all for coming today." Beth turned away from the lectern and hurried to the elevator. Barry and Jenny followed close behind.

* * *

Beth called Emma the moment she stepped inside Barry's apartment.

"Beth!" Emma answered, her voice carrying over the speakerphone. "I'm so glad you called."

"I just heard the news. Kayleigh fell and had surgery?"

"Yes. I'm sorry I didn't call you myself. Everything happened so fast."

Beth set her phone on the counter and settled onto a stool. "There's no need to apologize. You had more important things on your mind."

Emma sniffed. "I've never been so frightened in my life. I was in the kitchen when I heard a crack followed by a thump. When I ran into the bathroom, Kayleigh was already unconscious. I made sure she was breathing and called an ambulance. If she'd stopped breathing, I don't know what I would've done. With her neck the way it is, CPR can be risky. Fortunately, the EMTs arrived quickly and rushed her to Abbott Northwestern Hospital."

"Is she going to be okay?"

"She got the surgery we were all fighting for. That's the good news. Whether there will be bad news to go along with it is still to be determined."

"Bad news?"

"She could end up partially paralyzed, or worse."

"Oh, that poor girl."

"Right now, the surgeon is being extra cautious and has her in a medically induced coma."

"For how long?"

"I don't know. All he said was that it should be less than twenty-four hours."

"Is there anything we can do to help?"

"At this point, just knowing you care is enough."

"Then please keep us informed as you are able."

"I will."

Beth hung up and looked Barry in the eyes. "That dear girl has been through so much."

He frowned. "We're witnessing a variation of America's license to kill laws."

Beth tilted her head. "What do you mean, license to kill?"

"If you or I shot and killed just one person, we'd go to jail for the rest of our lives. Yet every day greedy corporations kill multiple people slowly and legally. All it takes for their license to kill are bribes to politicians for the elimination of safety and environmental regulations—or as they disingenuously call it, 'red tape.' It's the same thing for Kayleigh. If you or I pushed her in the bathroom, and she ended up paralyzed, we'd go to jail. In this instance, regulatory loopholes allowed Carephyx Healthnyt to delay Kayleigh's medical needs without consequences, leading to their virtual push in the bathroom. Now, even if she ends up paralyzed, no one will go to jail. The consequences for Carephyx Healthnyt will, at worst, be that they finally have to pay for the surgery they had previously declared to be elective."

"I agree," said Beth. "It's a tragedy that we live in an era where politicians get away with going on and on about what a great country we are, yet so many of the laws they pass favor corporate profits over people. Until voters collectively demand for that to change, everyday people will be shit out of luck."

"Knowing all that, if Kayleigh ends up paralyzed, I will forever wonder if we could have done more."

"Like what? Kill Edward Thomas? All that would've done is allow someone with a similar mindset to climb the corporate ladder and replace him."

Jenny spoke up. "Actually, our biggest mistake was believing we could shame a corporation into behaving ethically. Barry, if you're determined to beat yourself up over this, here's a better reason. We could've put our efforts into fundraising and paid for Kayleigh's operation before she fell."

Barry buried his face into his hands. "Then we're just as much to blame for what happened to Kayleigh as Carephyx Healthnyt is."

Jenny reached across the counter to put a hand on Barry's arm. "No. You were—we all were—thinking too big. We never spoke of it openly, but until now, nothing had ever stopped the Silver Squad from achieving success. Let's take some satisfaction in knowing that at least we tried."

He looked up. "I hate letting the bad guys win."

Jenny continued in a reassuring voice, "Ultimately, Kayleigh's fall will force Carephyx Healthnyt to pay her medical bills; likely more than they would've paid had they not delayed until the operation became an emergency. And if for some reason they don't cover everything, we'll do what we should've done in the first place."

"Fundraise," Barry said softly.

CHAPTER 36

The Drag Show

For the rest of the day, Barry, Beth, and Jenny remained in the apartment. Everyone kept their phones on as they waited for an update from Emma and answered calls from reporters who were requesting interviews or seeking replies to follow-up questions. Ultimately, those calls were a welcome diversion that made time pass quickly. Even Barry, who often ranted, "How the hell did that reporter get my number?" chatted to the media without complaint.

All the while, Beth resisted the urge to don a coat and drive to the hospital. She was in the bathroom when her resistance weakened, and she reasoned it wouldn't hurt to at least give Emma a call. She was about to do that when her phone chimed. "Emma! I was just thinking about you. Please tell me you have good news."

"Right now, I only have neutral news. Even though Kayleigh hasn't had any setbacks, her doctor has decided not to wake her until tomorrow morning."

"Would you like some company while you wait?"

"That's sweet, but my mother is here, and she's insisting that I head home to get some sleep. So that's what I'm gonna do. Tomorrow could be a long day. No matter what happens, your presence will be more valuable then."

"We'll all be there."

"I'll call you when I have a specific time."

"Okay. Give my best to Kate."

"I will."

After returning to her stool at the kitchen counter and relaying to Barry and Jenny the news from Emma, Beth asked, "Under the circumstances, should we postpone going to Harry's show and catch it some other night?"

Jenny set down her cell phone. "When we're done with our hospital visit, I've gotta return to Des Moines to get my life and business back in order. So, if one or both of you are game, I'd still like to go tonight."

Barry glanced at his watch. "I'm game. But if we're going out for dinner beforehand, we should leave within the hour."

Barry and Jenny tilted their gazes toward Beth.

Raising her palms like a preacher, she said, "I wasn't saying that I didn't wanna go. I was only checking to see if everyone else still wanted to go." She grinned. "Goth anyone?"

"Um . . . no," Barry said. "I'm not going to embarrass Harry by showing up wearing as much makeup as he has on. But if you ladies wanna do your Siouxsie Sioux thing, that's up to you. You'll probably fit right in."

"Are you sure you don't mind?"

"It's not what I think. It's what Harry would think. No son—no matter how old—wants a parent to embarrass him. When I worked in radio, I made quite a few public appearances, usually DJing at nightclubs. If my father had shown up at any of those events dressed in punk rock leather or, even worse, disco elephant bell jeans, I would have crawled under a table. What anyone accompanying him wore would have been irrelevant to me. Unless, of course, his companion was my mother."

Jenny smiled. "I don't know Harry very well, but I think he'll be so touched by your showing up that your outfit could consist solely of a Speedo and he wouldn't care."

Beth raised a hand. "But I would!"

Jenny giggled. "Okay, let's all wipe that image from our minds. . . . Beth, as long as Barry thinks our dressing up won't embarrass Harry, I'm all for it. We've experienced a lot of stress recently, and cutting loose could be just what we need."

Barry looked Jenny in the eyes. "You realize that if you two go crazy on the dance floor tonight, it'll be the women, not the men, who will be hitting on you."

Jenny waved a dismissive hand. "If you'd seen even a fraction of the men who've hit on me over the years, you'd know what a refreshing change of pace that'll be."

* * *

With eager anticipation of an evening free from abductions, guns, and high-speed driving, the three friends began preparations without delay. Even though Barry refused goth makeup and Robert Smith hair, he consented to wearing the all-black outfit Beth had purchased for him before the mass-shooting incident that made them famous. The women, on the other hand, looked fabulous all gothed up!

Their evening began at a French restaurant selected by Jenny. Despite their collective appearance, no one gave them a second glance. If they had wanted to attract attention any-where near Hennepin Avenue, they would've had to work much harder than they did.

From there, they strolled two blocks to the Gay 90s. None of them had patronized a gay bar before, but any apprehension they might have felt melted away when Harry met them at the door and began introducing them to his friends.

Earlier, Barry was unsure whether to surprise Harry with their visit or alert him ahead of time. Ultimately, he decided against the surprise, both out of respect and to learn Harry's performance schedule. Now he was confident he'd made the correct decision. In fact, as the two men were texting back and forth about their plans for the night, they had come up with a surprise for the women.

As is typical of such shows, multiple drag queens would perform that night, alternating songs through multiple sets. For much of that time, Barry sipped a drink in the back, watching Jenny and Beth dance with pretty much everyone. He soon gave up on trying to determine whether their partners were male, female, or something else. As he saw it, all that really mattered was that everyone was enjoying themselves. The only time he felt uncomfortable was when he found himself admir-ing a gorgeous woman, only to realize the object of his stare was actually a man.

Harry instigated the first surprise of the night. Upon seeing his father in the shadows, he talked one of the performers—a willowy blonde who had recently lip-synced a Lady Gaga num-ber—into pulling Barry onto the dance floor when the DJ was playing music between sets. Barry considered resisting before chugging the drink he'd just received and concluding that re-sistance would be more awkward than dancing. Although he didn't recognize the song, the beat was easy to follow, allowing him to mimic the moves of his dance partner. By midway through the song, he noticed that all the other dancers had stepped back to watch and exaggerated his moves further. As the two dramatically different men took over the dance floor, Barry flashed back to a wild party from his college days and prayed his recovery in the morning wouldn't be as painful as the one from that party, long ago.

The surprise for Beth and Jenny waited until Harry's final number, a song he added to his show at Barry's suggestion. When the unmistakable opening beat of "Slowdive" by Siouxsie and the Banshees filled the room, Beth erupted into a loud cheer. And when Harry pranced onto the stage wearing a spiky black Siouxsie Sioux wig, she turned to Jenny and let out a scream worthy of a sixteen-year-old groupie.

Barry laughed, enjoying the sight of Beth releasing her inner teenager.

Harry waved for Beth and Jenny to approach. As he pulled them on stage, he put his lips to Beth's ear and asked, "Have you seen the video for this song?"

"Of course!" she exclaimed.

"Then you know what to do."

Even though the video was popular well before Jenny's time, when Beth mouthed to her, "follow me," hunched over behind Harry, and began swinging her arms and stepping to the beat, she quickly caught on.

When the song faded, Beth's shout of "That was so much fun!" rose above the wall of applause.

Harry collected his tips, leaving numerous hands waving in the air. "Those are for you and Jenny," he said to Beth as he escorted her back onto the dance floor.

* * *

As the crowd thinned, Harry joined Barry, Beth, and Jenny at the bar for a nightcap, funded by the women's unexpected tips. "You ladies can join me on stage anytime," he said. "Both of you were amazing!"

"Are you sure you're not just saying that?" Jenny asked. "We were behind you for the entire song. We might've sucked."

"I watched a video of it backstage. I'll email you a copy."

Barry gave everyone time to finish their drinks before announcing, "We'd better head home. Tomorrow could be a long day."

Harry reached out to pull Barry into a hug. "Thanks for coming, Dad. It meant a lot to me."

"Of course, son." He sniffed. "I'm so goddamn proud of you."

Harry held the hug for a moment before parting with a rapid set of pats and turning to exchange hugs with Beth and Jenny.

As the three friends stepped outside, the biting wind that greeted Barry was unable to chill the warm feelings that were immobilizing his vocal cords. That same wind seemed to encourage Beth and Jenny to chat all the way to the Mustang—and ultimately all the way to the Blue Loon Village. That Barry never had to utter a word was just fine with him.

CHAPTER 37

Grandpa Barry, Grandma Beth, and Auntie Jenny

Beth's phone rang midway through breakfast. It was Emma. "The doctor has begun the process of waking Kayleigh. It'll be a few hours before you'll be able to see her, but you're welcome to come by anytime."

"Thanks for the heads-up. We'll drive over after breakfast. Where should we meet you?"

"Send me a text when you arrive, and I'll let you know."

* * *

Upon reaching Abbott Northwestern Hospital, Beth exchanged texts with Emma and led her companions to the waiting room closest to where Kayleigh was located.

Emma stood as the Silver Squad walked into the room, and for the first time since they'd met, she greeted them with a wide smile. "I have encouraging news! Kayleigh is already awake. The doctor came out and spoke with me a moment ago. He says she will have a long healing process ahead but doesn't appear to have any paralysis."

Beth beamed. "What a relief!"

"When can we see her?" Barry asked.

"We all have to wait until the doctor finishes his examination." She motioned toward a line of five unoccupied chairs. "I don't think it'll be too long."

Once everyone selected a seat, Emma began sharing the details of Kayleigh's operation and what was ahead for her recovery.

Emma's mother, Kate, joined them in mid-conversation, settling into the remaining chair with a cinnamon roll and coffee she'd purchased in the cafeteria. She exchanged greetings with everyone before saying, "I've already heard all this, so there's no need to catch me up."

Shortly thereafter, a sturdily built nurse entered the waiting room to escort Emma and Kate to Kayleigh's room. When Barry, Beth, and Jenny stood to follow, the nurse flashed her palm. "Immediate family only at this time. If the patient isn't too exhausted after their visit, I will come and get you."

Returning to his chair, Barry thumbed through a pile of old magazines. Finding none that interested him, he tilted his head toward Beth and said, "I'm at the point in my life where I'm not quite sure how to handle waiting. Should I be relaxed about it, because I'm retired without pressing obligations? Or should I be tense about it, because I'm wasting the precious time I have left?"

"It's the septuagenarian's dilemma," she replied.

Jenny leaned forward in her chair. "I don't know anyone

who enjoys waiting, but no matter how long we have to wait here, it'll be far less than the years of waiting Kayleigh had to endure."

Barry scoffed. "I bet the top executives at Carephyx Healthnyt won't have to wait long for their next bonus."

Jenny nodded. "Well, ya know, once people motivated by extreme greed acquire more money than they can possibly spend, it just becomes a game for them. He who dies with the most money wins."

"The fuckers!" Barry blurted.

"Shhh!" A curly-haired woman hissed from the opposite side of the room. "There are families in here."

"Sorry!" Barry exclaimed, clapping a hand over his mouth.

Jenny sucked in her lips, trying not to laugh.

The waiting room reverted to hushed conversations until Emma and Kate returned with the nurse.

Emma grinned. "Next?"

The Silver Squad followed the nurse down a long hallway.

Barry playfully shielded his eyes as they entered Kayleigh's room. "That smile! I've never seen anything so bright! Did you swallow a flashlight?"

Kayleigh giggled. "Very funny, Grandpa Barry." Her eyes shifted to the women. "Grandma Beth! Auntie Jenny! The doctor says I might be able to go back to school next year!"

Beth swept her gaze across Kayleigh—her body still attached to tubes and monitors; her neck remaining in a stiff brace—and willed herself not to cry tears of conflicting emotions. She grasped Kayleigh's hand. "That's the best news ever, dear!"

Jenny circled around the bed to take Kayleigh's other hand. *"Auntie Jenny,* huh? I've never been anyone's aunt before. What are my responsibilities?"

"Well, first you need to take me skiing when I'm all better."

"What kind of skiing—water, downhill, or cross-country?"

"Um . . . we'd better go cross-country. My mom would freak if I did anything else."

"Okay. I can do that."

"And after that, you need to . . ."

ABOUT THE AUTHOR

The author on stage at Northwestern Michigan College

Marty Essen grew up in Minnesota and resides in Montana. In addition to being an author, he is also a talent agent and a college speaker. Since 2007, Marty has been performing *Around the World in 90 Minutes* on college campuses from coast to coast. *Around the World in 90 Minutes* is based on his first book, *Cool Creatures, Hot Planet: Exploring the Seven Continents,* and it has become one of the most popular slide shows of all-time.

Please enjoy all of Marty Essen's books:

Cool Creatures, Hot Planet: Exploring the Seven Continents
Six-Time Award Winner. Features 86 photographs.

Endangered Edens: Exploring the Arctic National Wildlife Refuge, Costa Rica, the Everglades, and Puerto Rico
Four-Time Award Winner. Features 180 photographs.

Time Is Irreverent
An irreverent, liberal, twisty, time travel comedy.

Time Is Irreverent 2: Jesus Christ, Not Again!
Another irreverent, liberal, twisty, time travel comedy.

Time Is Irreverent 3: Gone for 16 Seconds
Yet another irreverent, liberal, twisty, time travel comedy.

Time Is Irreverent: Ooh, It's a Trilogy! (Books 1-3)
The entire beloved series in a single e-book.

Hits, Heathens, and Hippos: Stories from an Agent, Activist, and Adventurer
A humorous memoir, with rock 'n' roll, headhunters, a demon-possessed watch, and a hippo attack.

Doctor Refurb
An unconventional, satirical, controversial, time travel comedy.

The Silver Squad: Rebels With Wrinkles
The eight-time award-winning first book in the Silver Squad series.

For information on Marty Essen's speaking engagements, please visit www.MartyEssen.com. For beautiful nature photography and biting political commentary, please visit www.Marty-Essen.com. To purchase signed copies of Marty Essen's books, please email Books@EncantePress.com.

PLEASE REVIEW THIS BOOK

Reviews are important! If you enjoyed *The Silver Squad Rides Again*, please post a review on the website of the retailer where you purchased this book. Thank you.